Bella

The story of an immigrant girl

a novel by
GEORGE ROGER RICHARD LE PORTE

PublishAmerica
Baltimore

© 2011 by George Roger Richard Le Porte.
All rights reserved. No part of this book may be reproduced, stored in a retrieval system or transmitted in any form or by any means without the prior written permission of the publishers, except by a reviewer who may quote brief passages in a review to be printed in a newspaper, magazine or journal.

First printing

This is a work of fiction. Names, characters, places, and incidents either are the product of the author's imagination or are used fictitiously. Any resemblance to actual persons, living or dead, events, or locales is entirely coincidental.

PublishAmerica has allowed this work to remain exactly as the author intended, verbatim, without editorial input.

Hardcover 978-1-4626-2015-9
Softcover 978-1-4626-2016-6
PUBLISHED BY PUBLISHAMERICA, LLLP
www.publishamerica.com
Baltimore

Printed in the United States of America

Bella

The story of an immigrant girl

Clipety clop, clipety, clop, clipety clop.

The noise from the wheels of the train lulled Bella into a reverie that took her back to the days just before the family had fled from their village.

The dreaminess of her reverie brought her to the noise outside their cottage in southern Russia on that fateful night of the slaughter.

The cacophony of the train's wheels reminded Bella of the same clipety clop noise of the horses' hooves on the cobblestoned road just outside of their cottage the night the Cossacks raided their tiny unprotected village.

Bella, that night, had wanted to see what it was that was making such a tremendous noise outside in the road.

She peeked out from behind the shutter and saw six gigantic steeds galloping three abreast, the whole width of the cobblestoned road, in front of their hut.

The animals were snorting icicles from their nostrils as a result of the cold weather outside. Astride these giant steeds were the largest Cossacks she had ever imagined. They were dressed in bearskin robes. Their heads were adorned with fur hats. Their beards and mustaches, Bella imagined, were meant to keep them warm as well, since ice patches were embedded into their hair. Icicles dripped from their nostrils, too. Their eyes looked like burning coals in the moonlit night. Crisscrossed from one shoulder to the other were wide leather straps holding the cartridges that went into the rifle they carried in one hand while wielding a saber in the other.

Their neighbors' homes were being invaded. Screaming neighbor women and children were terrified as their men ran out into the road trying to flee for their lives. The horses were too quick for them. The sabers did their work cutting down these helpless and defenseless villagers.

Horses were racing at tremendous speeds up and down the streets of the village. Right here in their village, just outside their door, you could hear more screams of their friends and neighbors being brutalized and attacked. The horses were actually knocking down the doors of their neighbors' huts as the Cossacks rode their giant steeds into the huts.

Bella's grandfather was shepherding the family down the steps to the underground room he had built anticipating just such a day as this.

Grandfather grabbed Bella in time and almost threw her down into the abyss. Grandfather had fixed the kitchen table so that it stood right over the trap door making the room look bare. Mama had snatched her Menorah candleholder and the silver teapot that she had received on her wedding day. It was the same teapot that was given to her mother and her mother before her. No one really knew how many years it had been in the family but everyone knew how important it was to Mama. The kids huddled against Mama terrified in fear of being discovered.

As Bella sat on the dirt floor with her mother and brother she remembered the warning and the stories grandfather used to tell after dinner as they all sat around the table.

He had told them that Jews were fair game for all of the radicals of the day. Pogroms took place in the towns and villages of southern Russia in an attempt to eradicate the Jews. There were as many as several hundred such attacks in a given year. Jewish men were killed and severely wounded. Their women were raped. Hundreds of thousands were left without homes and penniless. Not much was done by the local authorities. They had turned a blind eye to the plight of these poor folks. If they did act, the perpetrators were generally given a very light sentence for what they did.

To make matters worse laws forced Jews to return to the Pale, the Jewish ghetto, in many of the larger cities. All villages were ordered to expel Jews from their villages. The laws also limited the number of Jews who could attend secondary schools and universities grandfather said. The laws also prohibited Jews from becoming lawyers and restricted their ability to participate in government.

* * * * * *

All of a sudden Bella could hear that the front door had flown open. The cold air from outside howled as it swept through the crevices of their tiny shelter. The huddled family could hear the hooves of the horses above them. It sounded as though the marauders were drunk as they proceeded to smash what few treasures the family had kept stored in their cottage. The men upstairs, after a time, were certain that no one was in the house so they left.

Bella and her family stayed huddled all night long on the dirt floor for fear the men might return. The next morning they ventured out of the cellar and were able to see what had happened.

The chairs and table that Grandfather had whittled were broken. Everything was scattered and strewn as if a tornado had gone through their cottage. That was when Grandfather said to Mama, "Enough is enough. We must leave this place at once if the family is to survive. We will try to escape to America where my brother Leibish is already living. We will join with the others who are trying to get out of here."

"I have heard stories," he said. "Two and a half million Jews have already left the Pale and have gone to Eretz-Israel or to the United States. Since my brother Leibish is already settled in America we will go there!"

That morning grandfather found two neighbors who had survived the onslaught. Grandfather convinced them to go along with us. One of the neighbors had a cart with a donkey that was still alive.

The women and children rode in the cart, along with the provisions while the men walked alongside.

The first night was the scariest. It was the first time that the women and children had slept under the stars. Through the darkness the children could hear the howls of wolves in the distance. However, grandfather had assured everyone that as long as they stayed together near the fire they would not be attacked.

On another night, grandfather and the men came across a friendly farmer who allowed them to spend the night in his barn. The farmer's wife brought fresh goat's milk for the children while the farmer gave them a chicken to roast. Everyone was happy and relaxed. They were able to sleep in the warm, soft hay instead of the hard ground of the previous nights. It was nice to know that there were still good people who cared.

Another time, they camped near the woods. Grandfather took Abraham with him to look for game. Everyone was ecstatic when he reappeared with enough rabbits for all to feast on.

* * * * * *

It was a hazardous journey across the cold, snow-covered and hardened land. Drifts were sometimes higher than some of the children. The group of émigrés traveled mostly by night. Grandfather had warned everyone not to talk to anyone and to not trust a soul. The children were all warned about the robbers who prey on those émigrés trying to escape. "If we are stopped by brigands you are to lie still and not to move," Mama said. "Grandfather will speak for all of us." "No matter what, we are not to become separated," grandfather warned.

Mama had sewn some coins, she had saved over the years, into our coats. We were told that if anything had happened to any of the adults the children, with Bella in charge, were to follow Grandfather's instructions and try to get to Hamburg, Germany as quickly as possible. The coins would see them through. Fortunately, that eventuality had not happened.

As they neared the city of Hamburg they could see a railroad train in the distance along with smoke billowing from its stack. On the horizon the band of travelers could begin to see the outline of the buildings that made up this large city. What a relief!

They all had managed to get to Hamburg, Germany where they had been told they could find a ship that would take them through to the rest of their journey.

They were told that the great steamship company *Hamburg-Amerikanische Packet-fahrt Acten Gesellschaft* (HAPAG), would be the place where they would find the ship that would take them to America.

When they arrived at the port and found the ship that would take them to America, they discovered that there would be a fourteen-day period of quarantine. Papers needed to be checked and there was also a need to be certain that none of these immigrants had diseases that would spread. Grandfather checked in with the agent in charge and after registering the entire family talked with mama about his plan for them.

The rest of the people who had traveled with them were moaning and crying out that they were tricked and would never be allowed to leave. Grandfather didn't listen to their cries. He gathered us together and led us to a family that he knew.

When he was a youngster, he told us, he and his father had helped this family, the Rosens, settle in Hamburg. That is how he knew about the ship that would take us all to America.

Mr. Rosen was in the cheese business. Even though Mr. Rosen had a few goats of his own he looked forward to the quantities of milk that great grandfather brought to him. They developed a great relationship inasmuch as both grandfather's father and Mr. Rosen were honest tradesmen.

The Rosen family greeted us openly. Mrs. Rosen and her children ushered us into their house. We were introduced to everyone and were soon to sit down to a warm meal. Mrs. Rosen's comment was, "there's enough to feed everyone in my pot!" After dinner Grandfather and Mama gathered around the kitchen table with Mr. and Mrs. Rosen. Grandfather told them about our trek across Germany. The children were ushered into another room in order to sleep. Even though Bella and Abraham slept on the floor, it was warm.

The next day Grandfather helped Mr. Rosen with some of the outdoor chores while Mama and the children helped indoors. Mr. Rosen had some goats. He would milk them and make cheese. When the cheese was aged and ripe he would load up his wagon and peddle the cheese throughout the streets of the city. Mr. Rosen's cheese was very popular. The people, by now, had come to know that the quality of his wares was the best and that they would not be cheated either in price nor quality. After two weeks grandfather alerted the family and told them that they were finally allowed to take the ferry to a ship awaiting them in the harbor.

GEORGE ROGER RICHARD LE PORTE

* * * * * *

Bella wondered which was worse, that terrible night of the pogrom, the trek to Hamburg, or the trip to America.

They were escorted down into what seemed to be the deepest, dankest, bowels of the ship. The steps were a dirty looking steel with no handrails to hold on to. You had to put your hands along the walls that the sailors called bulkheads so as not to fall. The place that they descended into was called steerage. All of the people who were traveling, as cheaply as they could afford, were cramped into steerage. They numbered approximately four hundred. They were strangers from all over Europe. Each person received a place of about two feet wide and six feet long. This was to be home for the next two months!

The food people brought with them in order to sustain them during the trip was already beginning to rot and smell. If that wasn't enough, the stench of the body odors from the people brought on a constant state of nausea and the result was vomiting from day until night.

Seasickness, fever, dysentery, headache, heat, constipation, boils, scurvy, mouth-rot, lice and the like abounded. There was little or no light, ventilation or bathroom facilities. Some of the passengers relieved themselves in "thunder mugs" that they had brought with them.

If you had wanted to get away from the filth and the stench there was one small deck constantly awash with seawater. But despite the hazardousness of the situation it always provided some relief from the inhumanity of the compartment by breathing in the fresh clean smell of the salty sea air. It was especially pleasant when you saw the moon reflect off the waves that splashed alongside the ship and the stars that gave you hope of a better day to come.

Bella especially remembered the baby that was born amid this filth to a young girl who slept not more than ten feet away from her. The screaming and writhing of the pregnant woman's body sent a chill throughout Bella's bones. Everyone in the close compartment felt the pain that the girl was in. When the baby finally did arrive the mother grasped her to her waiting bosom and said, "She will be free. She is an American," Everyone cheered!

On the other hand, Bella recalled some of the sailors talking about the fact that children below the age of five rarely survived the voyage. This was sharply seen when many a mother was cast into the ocean with her child, as soon as it was dead, because they couldn't bear to live any longer without the young one.

One young girl who was to give birth and couldn't, under the circumstances of the filth and crowded and unsanitary conditions died. She too was thrown into the sea.

Bella overheard many of the older folks moaning and lamenting, "O God, why did you let me leave my home?" "The pig sty was better than this!"

Bella also recalled the woman who wore a striped shawl that resembled a *tallith,* a Jewish prayer shawl that was to be used only by the men to wear. This, to Bella, was a symbol of hope for their family as they prepared to arrive at their final destination.

GEORGE ROGER RICHARD LE PORTE

Thieves were everywhere within those small quarters. Mother was constantly warning us to watch our belongings, especially our coats in which she had sewn what few coins she had saved, not knowing how useful they would become in their new found land. We were lucky, remembered Bella. More lucky than some others who, during this long and arduous trip, had much of their treasures stolen.

There was an impatience clouding over the huddled masses of people in those cramped quarters. There was cruelty among them. The strong fed on the weak. Sometimes even killing one another. Husbands carped at wives. Wives carped at husbands and children. While those who had no one else to share their feelings with were heard to whimper, sigh and cry piteously. There was so much despair that it was nearly impossible to console the miserable ones.

When the ship arrived into New York Harbor it gave hope to everyone standing along the ship's railing. Their faces showed a look of promise although you could also sense a feeling of uncertainty about the future. Many began to weep for joy, some prayed, others sang thanking God and giving praise for having survived the ordeal. People came to life once again. It was as if a fairy godmother had waved her magic wand over this pitiable mass of humanity.

The daybreak of a bright autumn morning beamed over the magnificent Bay of New-York City as the ship carrying these immigrants from the Old World, fired a salute and cast anchor amid the ringing cheers of passengers and crew. It was indeed exhilarating, after days and nights of endurance in steerage and on deck, with the ever-same boundless blue and green of the sea, with only now and then a ship in sight, or the wild wheeling sea-gull on the vessel's track, to come in view of something like land.

It was sunrise in the New World! A glorious and electrifying sight it was, as the sun, about to rise on the horizon, flooded the bay. A billowy clouded, sky, overhead accentuated the surrounding scenery with streaks of gold and purple – New York City itself, and its sister cities of Brooklyn and Newark, New Jersey were just waking up out of the dreamy darkness of the night.

The great City of New York was exhilarating to see before them. The approach to New York was truly breathtaking. The immigrants saw steeples atop churches, public buildings, factories, stores, and other structures, as they steamed up the Bay.

The place where they had now arrived at, Castle Garden, attracted particular attention. This was the principal and most important stop, in all probability, for the emigrants.

Rumors and soft whispers began to circulate among the arrivals. Although its purpose now was that of an immigrant depot, it was an old fortress and castle they had heard about from among the crew.

The British built this castle in 1812. The building of red granite was of tremendous thickness, circular in form, and furnished with portholes and platforms, so that it would be available at any moment for the defense of the harbor.

After the War of 1812 when the peace and prosperity of the City were at its height, the building was converted into a saloon for the amusement of the people. It had held as many as 4,000 people, when Jenny Lind, the Swedish Nightingale performed there. But now this place represented a new beginning, a refuge for the strangers – men, women and children who come here year after year from afar to make a place for themselves in this new world across the sea.

A tugboat came alongside and was engaged for a considerable time in transferring the luggage of the first class passengers. Most of the immigrants carried what little they had.

Mama, grandfather, Bella and Abraham, her little brother, were safely landed on the threshold of Castle Garden, glad and grateful to set foot on the land of the free, and rest their weary limbs.

The landing dock was alive with the officers of the Immigration Commission and the Customhouse, engaged in their duties. The new arrivals could only wonder what lay ahead for them.

The immigrants proceeded in a body up the corridor into the interior of the building and there they were told to sit. Their boxes and baggage were sent to the luggage warehouses. In front of them, and in the center of the building, which was lit by a glass dome, stood a staff of some dozen gentlemen, all busily engaged in making arrangements for facilitating the movements and promoting the settlement of the newly-arrived immigrants. Each immigrant, man, woman and child, passed up in rotation to the desk and gave the registrar his or her name and destination, as a check against the manifest turned in by the Captain of the vessel.

One of the officers connected with the Bureau of Information mounted a rostrum, and addressed the assembled immigrants. He told them that the process might take some time. If they could afford it they could pay for accommodations. If not, they can find shelter under the roof of this building. "In the meantime the processing will continue as quickly as possible," he said "getting tickets for railway and steamer that will take you where you need to go."

There also were officers helping those who needed information regarding the best means of obtaining employment. A register was kept in the Intelligence Department of the Institution.

The Intelligence Department was crowded about by many of the immigrants. There they could obtain information as to probable situations without fee. They were told that after they left Castle Garden they would find that that information would cost them as much as $2 by the employment agents.

The office carefully supervised the dissemination of this information. People were told as to the suitability and respectability of the parties on both sides. "All this is well and wisely done for the protection of the emigrant, who would otherwise, if left to himself, become the prey of "sharpers," boarding-house "runners", "scalpers", and "leafers," said the registrar in charge.

Folks were also given the best and most expeditious routes to take, as well as facilities for corresponding with friends, and of changing money at the Bureau of Exchange.

Those who were ill or an invalid were at once sent to the State Hospital, where they were to receive medical treatment and general attention. If the illness or infirmity was of such a nature that it could not be treated the people would be sent back on the next ship they were told.

When one considered the hundreds of thousands of immigrants who came to America each year you had to admire the way these immigrants were treated at Castle Garden.

It was nearly evening before all the business connected with the immigration department was over and the immigrants began to settle down in their new locality.

Even though grandfather had the letter from Uncle Leibisch reporting that we had a place to go and a job was in sight, we had to be delayed due to the large number of people who were being processed that day. A polite officer told Grandfather and Mama that we were sure to be on our way by the next day.

The building was lit up with gaslights by now. They gave a more cheerful appearance to the interior, and enabled us to look at the scene before us. Most of the people were seated on the benches that had been provided. It was interesting to note how the people arranged themselves by their ethnicity. The Germans and Dutch, who formed by far the most numerous group, settled off into the eastern portion of the building, which is separated from the other sections that contained English, Irish, Scotch and French. Interestingly enough the men were on one side and the women on the other.

Two large iron coal stoves, between four and five feet high, threw out considerable heat. There was one at each end of the room.

In a far corner of each area was a stand where for fifteen or twenty cents you can obtain a half a pint of coffee, a roll, cheese or butter; but many of the immigrants appeared to prefer preparing their own tea and coffee, on the stoves, in tin utensils, they had brought with them,. There were two water taps and an iron ladle at each end of the room for drinking. There was nothing in the shape of wine, lager beer or spirits being sold upon the premises. This surprised many of the immigrants who were used to having a pint or two in the evening!

Two very civil and intelligent watchmen patrolled the area during the night, to keep order, and keep an eye on the needs of the immigrants.

One will not very readily forget his first nights' sleep at Castle Garden, Bella thought. Almost everyone slept on the floor. The hard boards were anything but a soft featherbed. Most of them could not afford a dollar for their bed and breakfast.

Even though they still had the coins that mama had sewn into our coats they were told by Mama that they must hold on to them for an emergency. They tried to sleep, but vainly.

There was a great deal of anxiety over what was coming next. One could hear a cacophony of many languages being spoken; the squalling of children and the erratic ramblings about of a colony of rats someone had seen. It was impossible to get some sleep, Many had become accustomed to the rocking to and fro of the reeling of the ship they had just left. Consequently the hard floor was not an adequate substitute!

Those who were unable to sleep rose and stood around the stoves. One subject of conversation dealt with the sadness related to those who perished during the journey. Others reminisced about their homes in the "old Country." They wondered if their new life would be worth the agony of their journey.

As might well be imagined, much of the conversation of the sleepless immigrants that night was directed to the good or bad fortune they had met with during the day in quest of situations and employment, Many came back reporting dolefully and despondently in that respect. Bakers butchers, boiler-makers, gardeners, grooms, and in fact masters of almost every calling to be found in the book of trades, all stated how they had canvassed the various establishments in the great City during the day, and had found, with some few exceptions, that they were all full, and that no help or hands were wanted. Never were the advertisement columns of the newspapers, for "help wanted," devoured with such avidness for the few cents invested in them. It was reported that some of the immigrants were sent, by order of the Commissioners, to Ward's island, to be employed in miscellaneous work at the State Hospital and grounds, or to work at their respective trades, for which they received their board and lodging in return, until something better could be obtained for them.

It was also rumored that most of the strong, healthy girls and young women, principally Irish, succeeded, through the agency of the Labor Department of the Commissioners, in obtaining situations as housemaids, nursemaids, milliners, sewing-machine hands and dressmakers.

There was also talk about a group known as the St. George's Society, who were on hand to help with assisting Englishmen upon their arrival.

At one time it was seriously contemplated by some of the more despondent and disappointed to turn "stowaway" and return from whence they came, in spite of being made the laughing-stock of those at home; and some half-dozen, who could not be induced "to wait a little longer," actually went back on board to return.

There was no prohibition against "smoking" at the Garden consequently many of the men were seen drawing on their pipe as being one of the prime comforts and companions of the poor immigrant during all of his "trials."

Morning arrived. After a few brief conversations with an inspector, grandfather shepherded us to the ferry that would take us to the train depot.

* * * * * *

Bella was jarred awake from her reverie when she heard the conductor shouting Binghamton! – Binghamton! – Next stop Binghamton!

She was in awe over the huge train yards she saw from her coach window. Railroad cars with strange names were sitting along the tracks. There were cars labeled New York, Lake Erie & Western; Delaware, Lackawanna and Western; New York Central; Utica and Susquehanna; Delaware and Hudson Canal Company; and many more. They all had strange names that made things even more confusing than ever. Bella wondered where all of these trains could possibly go.

When the train pulled to a stop at the station there was a great deal of excitement. The black man called a "Red Cap" put down a small stepstool so that the passengers could climb down from the car to the pavement. He even helped Mama with her baggage!

There he was, Uncle Leibish waiting to greet the immigrant family to America. He recognized Grandfather, Mama, Abraham, and Bella immediately from the many descriptions in the letters that had passed across the Atlantic since Uncle Leibish had gone to America. Uncle Leibish moved towards the group. There were hugs and kisses all over. They gathered their belongings and headed for the horse-drawn wagon that would take them to their new home. There were benches lined up on each side of the wagon for people to sit on. The driver collected the fare as each person boarded the conveyance.

Uncle Leibish explained that here in America what we once called a village was called a neighborhood even though villages did exist. Our neighborhood, he explained further, was a nice German-Jewish neighborhood. It seems that the immigrants tended to live in areas where others like themselves would be living. This made it easier for folks to assimilate into the mainstream of America, he said. You could buy groceries and meats similar to those you were familiar with in your home country. And, people spoke the same language you did so that you could learn to speak English at your own pace.

And, there were people who could understand you even if

you did speak a different language.

Churches and synagogues, too, had found their way into the neighborhoods. It was just like being in your own village!

Uncle Leibish then informed us that in America his name was changed to Louis. It was easier for folks to call him that.

The ride was interesting to Bella. The houses were not like those in the village from whence they came. These houses were "stuck" together. They had large steps in front of them. Uncle Louis had called them "stoops." And, they were several stories high! One of the main things that had caught Bella's eye was in the windows. The curtains were the same curtains that you would have found in the windows of her own little village. In many instances they were crocheted with the same familiar patterns that gave testimony to the fact that they had kept part of their heritage in tact in this new place called America.

There were stores among the houses. There were pushcarts up and down the streets with people selling fresh vegetables and ice. Can you imagine that! Bella had never seen ice being brought to someone's house before. Even though she had seen ice in the wintertime when things got so cold everything was frozen in the village she found it hard to imagine that ice could be delivered.

When Bella asked about this Uncle Louis explained that people kept an "ice box" in their apartment in order to keep their food fresh. The ice is stored in a compartment on top of the section where one stores the food they wish to keep. In America this kind of food was called. "leftovers." In addition they kept, milk, eggs, cheeses and a whole lot of other things.

The house Uncle Louis lived in was a three story building that was shared with five other families. Two families lived on each floor across the hall from each other.

This group of immigrants, in ignorant awe, trudged up the flight of stairs to the apartment rented by Uncle Louis and his family.

Aunt Sadie and the cousins greeted them at the door when the travelers got to Uncle Louis' apartment. They were told that they would be staying with Uncle Leibisch and Aunt Sadie until Grandfather and Mama could find some work and then Uncle Louis assured them that in no time they could have their own apartment, which would be soon.

Bella truly believed what Uncle Louis had been saying. Just by looking around the room called the kitchen area it seemed like magic. Against one wall was a coal stove with six holes for the coal and it had an oven!

Against the other wall was that magic box Uncle Louis had referred to on the trolley car ride – the Icebox. It was a wooden box of about three feet wide and six feet tall. When you opened the door Bella could see milk and eggs and meat and vegetables. It was a treasure trove of goodies. Over the large door was another smaller door. When you opened that one you could see a large piece of ice. Even though it was melting it was what was keeping everything cold. Aunt Sadie told Bella that the most important task for the kids was to check on the basin underneath the icebox. The basin collected the melted water. It was necessary to empty the water twice a day so that it didn't overflow onto the floor. The next room was a bedroom followed by another bedroom. Toward the front of the apartment was what Aunt Sadie referred to as the living room. There was a plush sofa covered with a huge hand-knitted afghan. There was also an elegant plush chair also covered with an afghan. End tables with crocheted doilies stood on either side of the chair and a small table was situated in the center of the room. Aunt Sadie explained that this room was only used when special company came to visit.

Uncle Leibish must be very rich, Bella thought, to be able to afford all of this!

That night mama helped Aunt Sadie make the dinner. They had potato soup with Nockerl, (the best kind of dumplings you could want, to go with the soup), Roast chicken with stuffed Helzel, and for dessert they finished with Mandelbrot. This surely was a feast! The weary travelers hadn't seen so much food in months. Not even in the best of times could they have expected a meal like this. It was fit for a king!

Uncle Louis said that even though the work is hard there is plenty of it for those who want to make a decent living. He added that the wages are good. You get a good day's wage for a good day's work! You can't ask for anything better.

After dinner, Mama and Aunt Sadie did the dishes while the kids went into the next room in order to get acquainted further. Everyone was stuffed from dinner.

The kids got together to play while the adults sat around the kitchen table talking. They talked about the good old times back at the village. But, they also talked about how things had gotten so bad that people were leaving because it had gotten so unbearable. Grandfather and Uncle Louis were sitting at the kitchen table and talking about the past and the future.

Grandfather had always worked with leather in his home village, he reminded Uncle Louis. Uncle Louis said that that was perfect because there was a big shoe company nearby that was always looking for good men who could handle leather well enough to make the shoes that they sold all over the country. Uncle Louis said enough of this kind of talk. He told Grandfather, "I'll take you down to see the foreman tomorrow. I'm sure he'll find a job for you." In the meantime let's celebrate now that you have all come to America. "Wait and see," said Uncle Louis, "you can't believe how much better life is here in America!"

We could hear Aunt Sadie telling mama, "Tomorrow we will bring the kinder to school." Here in America everyone has an opportunity to go to school. Wait, you will see, added Aunt Sadie.

* * * * * *

The next morning came early. It was 6 o'clock and still dark outside. Uncle Louis and Grandfather were finishing their coffee and the leftover Mandelbrot before leaving for work.

Aunt Sadie reminded us that if we needed to use the toilet we had to go out into the hall. Uncle Louis and Aunt Sadie lived on the third floor of this building. Each floor had two families living on it. There were bathrooms on each of the floors, out in the hall, for the families to use. The bathroom was very small. There was a commode and a sink. There was a bare bulb with a string hanging down from it so you could pull on the string to turn the light on and off. Over the door there was a transom so that the air could circulate. "At least we don't have to go outdoors in the cold to an outhouse," Bella said to mama.

After breakfast mama got the children dressed. Aunt Sadie had given mama some things for them to wear in order that they look most presentable for school. They were clothes that their cousins had outgrown. One thing was very important. Mama always said, "You must always be neat and dressed in clean clothes in order to be ready to learn." "What would the teacher think if you showed up in tattered rags and a dirty face," Aunt Sadie had said, "We must always show them how proud we are."

They walked the few blocks to school. The neighborhood was already astir. Adults were trudging off to work and kids were headed for school.

It seems as though each "neighborhood" had its own school. It was called a public school and had a number instead of a name. Bella thought that was very strange until Aunt Sadie pointed out that the city is very large. Numbers were the best and easiest way to keep track of them. The most important thing to remember was that it was a school and it was free for anyone who wanted to learn. Mama was impressed with what she saw. The building was huge. It was a concrete and brick building that was three stories high.. It was a far cry from the small wooden structure that stood in their village. There were steps leading up to the main entrance and the door was made of metal. When they arrived at the gate to the school-yard there were kids of all sizes and persuasions playing hop-scotch and jumping rope among other things. It seemed as though these children did not have a care in the world.

All of a sudden, out of nowhere a bell sounded and the kids began to scatter. They headed as fast as their legs could carry them to the inside of the building. They were going to their classes Aunt Sadie told Mama. Mama, Aunt Sadie and the new arrivals headed toward the principal's office. The cousins were already gone headed to the respective classrooms.

There was a large desk in front of everyone after the door was opened. Behind this barrier sat the secretary who greeted the group with a friendly smile. "So, these are the new cousins we're all waiting for," she said.

Aunt Sadie informed Mama that she had visited the school to make sure that they would be ready for the kids. Aunt Sadie and Mama sat down in the Principal's office while Abraham and Bella sat on large sturdy oak chairs in the secretary's office.

The principal was a kindly lady. She had already made plans that were discussed among the adults. After meeting with the Principal, Miss Smith, it was decided which grade to put the children in. Because the children could not yet speak, read or write English they were put into classes with the younger students. Bella was determined that she would learn as fast as she could so that she would not have to stay with the young ones for too long. It was easier for her brother since he was already young! They walked down the hallway. It was very quiet. They came to a door marked with a number 4. Bella was to start in the fourth grade while Abraham was shepherded into the 2nd grade. The principal led the way. When the door to the room was opened Bella was amazed at what she saw. Facing her on the outside wall were five windows with shades that pulled up and down in order to keep the sunshine in or out of the classroom. Underneath these windows stood the radiators that heated the room. This was nothing like the little wood-burning stove from the village she had come from. In the back of the room, against the wall, were book shelves full of all kinds of books, Bella was soon to learn that if you completed your class work early and got everything right you had the privilege of picking out your own book to read until the rest of the class "caught up." However, the thing that really impressed Bella was the table that sat in front of the bookcase. On the table was a plant and a fish tank with three goldfish swimming around in it. Bella also learned that if you were "good" for the day in the eyes of the teacher, you got to feed the goldfish. Along the inner wall was a chalkboard with a place for chalk and erasers to sit. Bella had never seen so much chalk before. In the village school they did all of their work in their little note pads. Again, Bella learned soon after that the "best" students each day were chosen to go outdoors into the schoolyard and "clap" the erasers. This was a very important job! Also, on this wall was a great big clock and next to the clock was an American flag. Each day the class began the day with a prayer and a salute to the flag with the children all reciting the Pledge of Allegiance. This was something totally new to Bella but she thought it was a great way to start. After all, she too was proud to be in the country of America. Bella could then observe the class seated in rows. They were quietly writing with their pens that they dipped into an inkwell situated in the far corner of the desk. Miss Smith introduced Bella to her teacher, Miss Westcott. Miss Westcott greeted them with a smile. She turned to the class and said, "Class, here is the little girl we've all been waiting for. I want you all to greet her with a warm hello," The class responded in unison with a "hello and welcome." It was obviously rehearsed, but Bella liked the warm feeling that she got, That helped her to overcome most of the fears that she held on to about whether they would be accepted or not.

There were about twenty-five students in the room that turned out to be a rather pleasant room. Across the front wall Bella could see the letters of the alphabet, both upper and lower case. She learned from her penmanship class that these letters were a part of the Palmer method of writing. Bella knew that she would learn to write as neatly and as quickly as possible.

Bella was assigned a seat, after she had hung her coat in the cloak room. The cloak room was a closet to the right of Miss Westcott's desk where each student had their own hook on which to hang their coat. Over each hook was the first name of each child. Bella found that there already was a empty hook with her name over it just waiting for her coat. Bella took her seat way in the back of the last row and the learning began. When the first week was over Bella discovered that the seating assignments changed. Students were assigned their seats according to their grades. The smartest student for the week sat in the first row first seat and the rest followed. Bella was determined that she would soon be sitting in that first row seat and that she would hold on to it. It was a great incentive.

Miss Westcott, Bella's teacher, found out that Bella was a quick learner and that she wanted to learn everything that she could learn as fast as she possibly could.

Miss Westcott was so impressed with what Bella had accomplished in the first weeks of her being in the class that she gave Bella extra assignments and took a special interest in her.

Bella was fascinated with all of the things that she was learning. The day was broken down into parts. There was always English and Mathematics, in the morning, every day. On some of the days you would learn all about Geography, or History. Bella especially liked the days when they had Music Appreciation and Art. In music appreciation they would listen to all kinds of classical music. The teacher always gave them a poem or rhyme to help them to remember the music with. Some of her favorites were, "this is the symphony that Schubert wrote and never finished," to the tune of the music. Or, "Barcarole from Tales of Hoffman written by Offenbach." They seemed to really fit and it surely made remembering much easier.

Some of the children hated those classes but not Bella. Music had always been a part of her life. Even in the village, whenever the folks in the village got together for some special day or event, out came the accordions and violins. Someone would always be playing an instrument of one sort or another. And, there was always grandfather with his violin. The men and women would sing and dance. It was always a fun time for Bella and all of the children of the village. These were some of the traits that Miss Westcott had picked up on.

Miss Westcott could see that Bella was a special student, bright, keen, and eager to learn. Miss Westcott told Bella that if she worked hard enough she could one day go to college and perhaps become a teacher like her. Bella didn't dare tell Mama and grandfather. Their future for her was to work in the cigar factory that Aunt Sadie worked in as soon as she got a bit bigger and had learned the language. Already, she was getting close to that age when she had to go to work. Mama and Aunt Sadie had both agreed that when Bella could speak English better she could then go to work.

* * * * * *

Miss Westcott had a younger sister close to Bella's age. With mama's permission Miss Westcott would take Bella to her home, after school or on Sunday afternoon, where she could play with Miss Westcott's sister Agnes.

Bella was in awe when they arrived at Miss Westcott's house. In Bella's eyes, the house was truly a palatial mansion! There were large white pillars on each side of the top steps leading to the front porch. Bella learned later that at the top of the pillars where it looked like leaves, Miss Westcott explained, that they were Corinthian-styled pillars. She went on to add that there are two other styles you can see in their neighborhood. "These styles," said Miss Westcott. "are called Doric and Ionic."

They walked up several steps to the front porch. On the

porch there was a glider and many hanging flower pots. Bella, again, gasped over the size of the house. It was a palace, she thought. It was huge for one family to live in, she thought. The Westcotts were the only ones who lived in the house that had ten rooms, two floors, a basement and an attic!

Then Bella spied the front door. The windowpanes in the huge door were etched with a picture of flowers in a basket and the solid door was made of oak.

The door opened into a huge vestibule. Bella noticed a huge vase filled with umbrellas just to the right of they door as they went inside. Above the umbrella vase was a section of wooden hooks made from oak where the children could hang their coats when they came into the house.

When they left the vestibule area they came to what was called a foyer with stairs leading up to the second floor. Every bit of floor was covered with carpeting. Bella had never seen anything as lavish as this before!

The room to the left of the stairway was the sitting room. Casual folks and business folks who came for a short time were ushered into that room if they had any business with the family. Behind the sitting room was a sliding door that stood between it and the dining room. Against one wall in the dining room was a huge buffet. In the buffet, Bella later learned is where the linen and lace tablecloths were kept along with the silverware and on top were beautiful silver candelabra. In a corner of the room there was a huge cabinet full of dishes. There were the everyday dishes as well as the dishes that were put on the table for special occasions. This was where the family was served their dinner by the maid who lived with them. The crystal glasses sparkled through the glass in the doors that closed on the cabinet. On each wall Bella noted the paintings of outdoor scenes showing flowers and waterfalls and green gardens. How beautiful and calming this room seemed to her.

The maid was a slight Black girl named Lilly. She was friendly and always wore a smile. Lilly always wore a black dress with a white lace collar and white-laced sleeves and a very white and starched apron. She was as neat as a pin, always! But, she only spoke when someone spoke to her.

Lilly and Bella became good friends as the weeks went on.

In the room to the right of the stairs was the parlor room. This room was for more formal company. This is where the family entertained their special guests, Bella was told. In the parlor was a beautiful Steinway piano along with stuffed chairs. All of the stuffed chairs had antimacassar crocheted doilies at the center of the backrest. All of the side tables were adorned with crocheted doilies, too. Hanging from the ceiling was a huge, glass chandelier. Bella was entranced by it all. It could have been a page from a storybook!

In the far wall there was a tremendous brick fireplace. Over the mantle there was a huge painting of Mr. Westcott's father. Bella couldn't understand why he wasn't smiling. Anyone who lived in a house like this should have been very happy!

It was there that Bella learned to play the piano. Miss Westcott encouraged her to take lessons when Miss Westcott's sister Agnes had her lessons. Mrs. Westcott was the teacher.

Agnes was not too interested in her lessons. Mrs. Westcott was only too happy to teach Bella. Bella had really wanted to learn! Music had always been an important part of her family's life. Grandfather would play his violin at holiday time. Everyone would sing and dance. Those were happy times. Music gave Bella sweet memories of times past.

Learning the scales was quite hard in the beginning. But, as they went along scales became easier. After a month or so Bella was already playing pieces. There was something about playing the piano that allowed Bella to drift off into another world. It was her escape from this world.

It was Lilly who also encouraged Bella to learn to play the piano well. Lilly told her that one day something nice would happen if Bella continued with her lessons and learned to play well. She told Bella about the evening recitals Mr. and Mrs. Westcott held from time to time. All of the "best" people in the city were invited!

It was not long after that when Bella had found out what Lilly was talking about when she made reference to the "best" people.

It was a Sunday afternoon in July. The Westcotts had invited the Woodruff's and the Lesters as well as other friends for an afternoon highlighted by a recital from Mrs. Westcott's piano students. Of course the featured pianist was to be Agnes although there were several others among the students. Before the recital, the adult men sat on the porch talking politics and business, the women sat chatting in the parlor while the children gathered in the yard with their pitchers of lemonade.

They played games until the time when the ritual called a recital had come due.

The yard was something to behold. The colors from all of the flowers were like an artist's palette. Joseph. Their Italian gardener looked upon them as his own little children. These beautiful flowerbeds flanked both sides of an elegant porch with a winding stairway down to a green lawn that looked like a carpet.

In the far corner was a gazebo situated behind a rose trellis. When you sat in the gazebo you could smell the aroma of the roses that adorned the trellis. Across from the gazebo the children had their croquet set and badminton court. There was always something for them to do!

Among the friends of Agnes was Richard Woodruff the son of Charles Woodruff. It became very clear to Bella that Richard had taken a fancy to her. Her friend Agnes told her all about Richard. Upon graduation from his prep school he would be attending Hamilton College located in Clinton, New York. His father wants him to be a business major with the thought that he might want to become a lawyer. His father had wanted him to become a lawyer and work in the family firm. Although the flirtation was harmless Bella had felt an attraction to Richard, too.

The highlight of the afternoon came when Agnes told her mother that she really didn't want to play at the recital because she had a splitting headache. She recommended to Mrs. Westcott that Bella could take her place. "After all," she said, "Bella is much better than I am." At the insistence of

Mrs. Westcott and the prodding of Miss Westcott Bella sat at the huge piano and played one of her favorites, The Barcarole from the Tales of Hoffman. When she was through everyone applauded and talked about how well she had learned such a difficult piece in such a short time. As Bella glanced across the room she could see Richard quietly mouthing the word, "fantastic!" Bella felt a rush come over her. Miss Westcott fawned over Bella for the rest of the afternoon before returning her to her home.

Miss Westcott stopped in to talk with Mama. She told her all about the afternoon and how Mama's daughter was such a big hit. Mama was proud and she told Bella how proud she was. When Miss Westcott left the apartment Bella sat down with Mama and related to her all the fantastic events of that afternoon. She never mentioned Richard, however. But, all in all, mama realized that this was a special treat for her daughter Bella.

That was the fun part of knowing and having Miss. Westcott as a teacher and a friend.

In the classroom it was a different story. It always seemed to Bella that Miss. Wescott was picking on her. She expected much more from Bella than she did of the other students.

If Bella were to tell this to Mama she knew she would be told that she should be thankful that Miss. Westcott had taken such an interest in her. Mama always said, "Bella, you must always be the best. An education is the most important thing in life. No one can ever take that away from you!

* * * * * *

GEORGE ROGER RICHARD LE PORTE

In 1857, Harvey Westcott employed about fifteen "hands" in the manufacture of cigars for the local trade as well as for jobbers. He had leased the upper part of the old Congdon Hall Block in the city of Binghamton, New York. And for his time, this was considered to be a sizeable venture.

Two years later, Mr. Westcott formed a partnership with Mr. George A. Kent who came to Binghamton from Monticello, New York. Together they retailed, as well as manufactured, cigars. In 1861, Mr. Kent took charge of a tobacco store in Scranton, Pennsylvania.

Prior to 1860 there were only four major manufacturers of cigars. The other three companies were Charles Butler, considered the pioneer of cigar making for that area; Lyman Clock; and Barlow and Rood.

Two factors were responsible for a fast, sudden change toward meteoric growth and expansion of this industry. Up until this time all of the cigars had to be rolled and shaped by hand. There was no mechanical device for doing this work. However, during the early to middle sixties, as the result of a strike on the part of workers over wages, Lyman Clock, a manufacturer, introduced a "molder" or "shaper" to the industry. Shaper-made cigars of a cheaper grade were found to sell well in the markets; hence, the use of "forms" in all the large shops became a general practice.

Another factor was the increase in the production of tobacco in and around the Binghamton area. The Chemung Valley, as far north as in parts of Onondaga County and the area known as Big Flats which consisted of the Southern Tier (Southern

BELLA

New York) and Northern Pennsylvania became known as the tobacco-raising districts. By 1865, the total amount of tobacco grown in this region amounted to eight million, five hundred seventy thousand, four hundred forty one pounds!

The upheaval in the South and the events leading up to the Civil War accounted for the increase of activity on the part of farmers to speculate on the growing of tobacco in New York State, Pennsylvania and Connecticut.

During this time the civil war had broken out in America. George Kent enlisted in the army, as a Colonel, in 1862. His tour lasted until 1863. But he made some very powerful friends, both in the business word and in politics while serving the cause.

Along with increases in the growing of tobacco as a cash crop there was another event that impacted on them. By 1894, the population of Binghamton spiraled and accounted for the significant rise in people available for employment in the cigar industry in the years to follow.

Wescott and his partner Kent were quick to grasp this new trend. They enlarged their factory and hired more people. They quickly discovered that women were a great source for their labors. Nearly one-third of the work force were women. Women started at the age of fourteen. This is what Bella had to look forward to.

* * * * * *

Mama soon found employment. With the help and recommendations of Miss Westcott she was introduced to some of the finest families in the greater Binghamton area.

Inasmuch as mama was without skills she and Miss Westcott had agreed that there was a need among the elite for someone who could clean a house for those folks who did not have a live-in housekeeper. Mama worked long and hard. She soon developed the reputation of being more than just a hard worker. Others wanted her to work in their homes too. Mama had a regular schedule. Later she began to do the washing and ironing for these families. Everyone liked the meticulous care that Mama took, especially in her ironing. They also liked the clean white look of the laundry. Some people said that it sparkled after Mama got through with it.

There were some benefits that went along with her job. There were times when the people would give her leftover food to take home. On other occasions Mama would bring home the hand-me-down clothes that either no longer fit the children in the families or they no longer wanted the clothes.

One day when Bella was at school she was mortified when a strange little girl came up to her and said, "You're wearing my dress! You must be the poor girl my mother talks about." Bella, in tears, ran home to tell this to Mama. Mama responded by saying that even though the clothes once belonged to someone else we could hold our heads up high because we were always neat and clean.

In the meantime Grandfather was able, with the help of Uncle Louis, to get a job at the Lester Brothers shoe factory. It was a large four-story building situated on the corner of Washington and Henry Streets. Primarily, Horace Lester controlled the firm.

BELLA

Lester had left his home in East Haddam, Connecticut, around 1850, at the age of thirty, When he arrived in Binghamton he had set up a retail shoe store. The business had grown to the point that he needed a partner. He found a willing partner by the name of John Doubleday. The two of them set up a custom shop on Court Street – one of the major streets in Binghamton.

The store consisted of shoes in the front and a cobbler's bench in the rear. The retail trade did not materialize as Lester had hoped. Customized shoes were not what people wanted at that time. The partnership with Doubleday had dissolved and Horace went into business with his brother George. It had become apparent to them that wholesale shoes, rather than custom work, was the way to go.

Their market included, in addition to New York and New England; Ohio and Illinois. In 1854 they established the firm of Lester brothers and Company.

With the influx of immigrants, manufacturing was blossoming into extremely productive and lucrative endeavors. The days of Master craftsmen and the apprentice system was all but over. Workers streamed into factories.

With the introduction of new machinery it was no longer necessary to hire skilled craftsmen. The invention of the stitching machine had the greatest impact on the industry. Prior to the invention of this machine, women would take the shoes home and sew them by hand. Hence, the term "homework."

The Civil War had put a tremendous strain on the production of shoes. There was an increased demand by the Northern army that helped to all but eliminate custom craftsmen and promote the increased use of machines.

Although Grandfather was a custom craftsman he swallowed his pride and went to work on the new bibbing and stitching machine that had been perfected by John Brooke Nichols. This new machine was capable of completing as many as eighty pairs of shoes in the length of time it used to take for one pair to be made by a skilled worker!

Hours were long and pay was low. But, as Grandfather said, "A job is a job!" He added, "the pay here is much better than we had had it in Mother Russia."

After several weeks on the job another worker approached Grandfather. He attempted to talk to grandfather about joining a union, that was already formed, to help protect workers and workers rights,.

"In an attempt to reduce wages," the man said, "employers began to replace skilled workers with unskilled operators and in the process reduced our wages. Unskilled labor worked on the machines. Wages were uncertain and falling. Employment was uncertain and sporadic. Out of this situation came our organization the Knights of Saint Crispin that was formed to protest management's abominable treatment of us.

This organization called the Knights of Saint Crispin was named after the Patron Saint of shoemakers. The organization is made up of workers employed in the manufacture of boots and shoes."

Newell Daniels a shoemaker from Milford, Massachusetts, organized the first lodge in March 1867. Nothing came of his desire to organize his union in Milford. He moved to Milwaukee, Wisconsin where his ideas became accepted.

The ritual and constitution he had prepared was accepted there by a group of seven shoemakers, and in four years this small group of craftsmen had grown into a large international organization.

The organization designed to be a trades union to secure good wages and to keep down the numbers of workers beyond what the community needed as well as to limit the number of "green laborers" into the trade had spread throughout the United States and Canada.

In 1867 the organization had established an International Grand Lodge located in Rochester, New York not far from Binghamton.

In 1869 the Knights had numbered 83,000 members. In its' prime, it has been said, the Knights of St. Crispin, in certain locations, made and unmade politicians. It established a monthly magazine for its' members; it started cooperative stores; and it fought, often successfully, against threatened reductions of wages. It was a force to be reckoned with.

However, due to factionalism, it was acknowledged to be dead in 1878.

Although the national movement was seemingly over twenty years earlier there were still pockets of workmen who clung to the basic beliefs of that movement. Local lodges still existed long after the parent organization had folded and they wanted to keep the basic premises of that organization alive. The Binghamton Lodge was one of those who clung to the ideals expressed by Daniels.

Grandfather listened very carefully. He was harangued day after day about joining. He was also told of the possibility of a strike. He was told that the low wages they were receiving should be increased. However, in Grandfather's mind the wages he was receiving were great compared to the "old country." As far as keeping the labor forces numbers down, Grandfather was quick to realize that he was one of the ones this man was talking about! After all hadn't he recently gotten his job? And, wasn't he what they called, a greenie, "A Greenhorn?"

One of the things that bothered Grandfather was the fact that this was such a secretive organization. You had to be invited to join. In addition to being secretive, Grandfather learned that there were oaths to be taken and initiations to go through in order to gain entrance into the union. It had almost reminded him of the bigotry demonstrated against his people in mother-Russia!

When he talked to Mama, Aunt Sadie, and Uncle Louis about what was happening at the factory they came to the conclusion that he should do nothing to jeopardize his job. After all, Mama and grandfather still needed to be dependant upon the graciousness of Uncle Louis and his family.

Family ties were strongly adhered to. The Sabbath was the day that was spent together. Grandfather and Uncle Louis went to temple. Grandfather wore the old *tallith* he had brought with him from the old country.

The women had prepared for their meal the day before and supervised the children while all read from the Torah.

BELLA

On other days, Grandfather and Mama would sit at the table and reminisce over the family and of the times gone by. They were grateful for the opportunity to be in America. They had now been here for almost two years now. They were grateful for the ability to be free to worship and to work. But, best of all they were happy that the children could go to school and become much better off than they were.

* * * * * *

Some months later, Uncle Louis announced that he and his family would be moving to a flat around the corner. Mama and Grandfather didn't know what to say. Uncle Louis went on to say that he had talked to Mr. Kanker, the landlord, and Mr. Kanker agreed that Mama and Grandfather and the children could stay on renting this flat after Uncle Louis moved.

They moved around the corner. Their flat was much larger than the former one. The bathroom was inside their flat. They no longer had to share their bathroom with another family. In the bathroom there was a huge bathtub standing on four claw-like feet. Aunt Sadie said the kids could come over on Saturday night and take their bath here while the older folks visited. The kids no longer had to look forward to the large copper tub that Mama washed clothes in when it became bath time.

In addition they had three bedrooms a kitchen and a parlor. Imagine all that room!

* * * * * *

Mama and grandfather got to know the neighbors quite well. Aunt Sadie told Mama and grandfather they were fortunate to have very nice neighbors and they got to meet them soon after their arrival.

There was a German family, the Salg's. Mr. And Mrs. Salg had a son Martin. Mr. Salg was a mechanic and Mrs. Salg looked after the neighbor's children while their parents went to work.

They later became known to Bella and Abraham as Tanta and Oheom, Aunt and Uncle. It seemed that everyone the family got to know well, out of respect, were referred to as Aunt and Uncle.

The other family were the De Phillipses. They became known to Bella and Abraham as Uncle Joe and Aunt Katherine. The children were told that Aunt Katherine was once a singer at the La Scala Opera Company back in her homeland of Italy. Here in America she belonged to a small touring company that put on operas throughout the northeast. She was gone a lot. Uncle Joe worked in a factory. He was a boiler-man. He tended the furnace. Lisa Ramilda, the eldest of the children was just like a mother to her younger brothers and sisters. She looked after all of them. There was Raymond, Albert, Josephine, Agnes, and Rose. The children got along beautifully with Bella and Abraham and the families looked upon the children as all belonging together.

* * * * * *

There were always wonderful smells coming from their neighbors' kitchens. In the afternoon, as the children came home from school you could smell the aroma of the freshly baked bread from Aunt Katherine's oven. All of the children were always invited into Aunt Katherine's kitchen where she would take freshly baked Italian bread out of the oven. Instead of butter she would cover the bread with an almost greenish colored olive oil sprinkled with salt and pepper and a little oregano. Sometimes she would squeeze tomatoes on the bread. It was delicious!

Weekends were even greater with the smell of tomato sauce that would be put over the pasta as well as the aroma of garlic. You could depend on that smell every Sunday. It seemed to be a ritual. The entire family went to church in the morning. After church the children would help in setting the table. There was always a linen tablecloth. The best dishes would be placed at the table and everyone sat down to a scrumptious meal. There was always chicken soup to start things off. Then came the boiled chicken after that came the pasta and meatballs. Along with meatballs was a delicious rolled beef called bracciole. The bracciole was filled with hard-boiled eggs, parsley, onion and garlic that was rolled up to look almost like one of the cigars that Aunt Sadie rolled out at the cigar factory. There was always a pitcher of homemade wine on the table. Even the kids could have some wine with dinner although two-thirds of the glass was filled with water.

Bella recalled the words of Uncle Joe who always said, "Men drink. Fools get drunk!" The meal was always concluded with fresh fruit. In fact, Uncle Joe would cut up his fruit, especially peaches, they were his favorite, and soak the fruit in his wine glass before he ate his fruit.

Their kitchen was an interesting one, too. There was always a coffee pot on the stove so that there would be a hot cup of coffee for anyone who just dropped in. On the kitchen table, in the center next to the sugar bowl, was a bottle of Anisette. It was to flavor the coffee, mostly for the men.

Each August, Uncle Joe would go down to the farmers market and buy the grapes to make the wine with. The big old barrels were in the back yard. Each year the ritual was the same. The press for the grapes would appear as if out of nowhere. He would hose down the barrels and fill them up with water and then let the grapes soak along with the sugar that he heaped on them. The children were told to be careful when they played so as not to interfere with the fermenting that was going on. After the fermenting, the wine would be put into gallon jugs or left in a barrel for the winter. There was always plenty of wine, enough to share with all the neighbors.

The aroma from Tanta Salg's kitchen was quite different. There was always the smell of onions being sautéed to go with the many fried meat dishes. The native German dishes always smelled so good. There were many kinds of soups. Erbensuppe mit Sauer Sahe (Green Pea Soup), Kartoffelsuppe (Potato Soup), and one of Bella's favorites, Leberklosschen (liver Dumplings). Then for a main dish there was Sauerbraten, a kind of marinated beef, schnitzel (a veal cutlet), Ochsenschwanz-Eintopf (Ox-tail stew). Potatoes (kartoffein), Rueben (Rutabaga), and red cabbage (rotkohl) were familiar staples. But the desserts were fantastic! Bella's favorite was Mrs. Salg's Apfelstrudel.

The kids were always welcomed into everyone's household. Even though they were three separate families you'd think they were all part of one.

BELLA

* * * * * *

Although education of the children was the avenue out of the working class this fate was not in sight for Bella. With the new apartment it was necessary to have another income to rely on in case something had happened to Grandfather's job or to Mama. It was determined that Bella would go to work in the cigar factory with Aunt Sadie and Abraham would stay in school, hopefully to go to college where he would have the opportunity of becoming a doctor or a lawyer one day.

* * * * * *

At grandfather's factory talk of a strike was looming overhead even though it was clear that the Constitution and By-Laws of the Crispen organization did not condone the practice of strikes. What did in fact provoke the Crispens was the fact that the company had recently replaced six skilled workers with twelve unskilled workers. The Crispens felt it would hurt the industry, and themselves if shoddy workmanship would throw good workmen out of work.

Grandfather was in a quandary. Even though a job was paramount to him he was not certain how he would be treated by his fellow workers if he had tried to go to work as a "scab."

"A "scab' is what one was called if they crossed the picket line to go to work," Grandfather told Mama one night as they were talking things over. Grandfather said they were already talking about these things at the factory and he was worried.

George and Horace Lester made it very clear that they "claim the right to run their shop in their own way."

In the face of all of this Bella found herself forced into a situation where she would have to leave school and go to work in none other than the factory of her mentor's father, George Westcott.

Miss Westcott pleaded with Mama to let Bella stay in school. She told Mama over and over again what a great student Bella was, how quick it was for Bella to learn. How it would be a waste to make her go to work in a factory. But, it was all to no avail. Mama explained that the family needed to have another income. Mama made it clear to Miss Westcott that Abraham would be the one to go to college. In the meantime Bella would help in the family finances by going to work. When the time had come Miss. Westcott made it clear to Bella that she could continue with her piano lessons and visit her home on Sunday afternoons when the factory was closed. Miss Westcott told Bella that she would always be there for her.

* * * * * *

Bella reported for work with Aunt Sadie. It was dark when they arrived at the gate entrance where many workers were lined up to go into the huge, dark ominous-looking factory that housed the cigar makers who worked for George Westcott. Bella followed the crowd. They came to a room with a half dozen light bulbs hanging from cords. The lights were scattered around the room. "This," Aunt Sadie said, "is the shaping room."

There were three long vertical windows at the far end of this brick room. At this time of the day there was little or no light coming from them. Aunt Sadie explained that is why there were the lights. But, as soon as the light comes in from the windows the lights are turned off.

There were a number of women already sitting at their tables on one side and men on the other. Tobacco leaves were in the center of the table that stretched from one end of the room to the other. The women were dressed in their long sleeved blouses that were tight fitting around the neck in the style of the day. They were wearing a plain canvas-type apron so that they wouldn't get their clothes discolored. They sat about six feet apart from each other. Across from them the men were seated, also wearing an apron, however their aprons had two-inch wide stripes and the aprons came down below their knees just as the ladies were. Under their aprons some of the men wore white shirts and some of them even wore a tie while others wore the traditional blue cotton shirt.

Aunt Sadie had been working as a shaper for some time and knew the foreman quite well. The foreman had decided that it would probably be best if Bella worked alongside of Aunt Sadie, as a shaper, to start with, until she was able to work on her own. Although the work was not very difficult, hours were long and tedious. Bella soon found that her fingers ached and the bones in her wrists were equally sore. There was always the quota to make each day if you wanted to continue to work at your job.

Bella was a quick learner after watching a number of 16 to 18-year old girls at their stations. Despite the damp tobacco atmosphere, Bella learned to get used to it. She paid close attention to what the girls were doing and how they did their job.

The core was made of filler tobacco, a cheap coarse tobacco rolled into proper shape. Then a binder was rolled on. This was followed by a final layer called the wrapper. The wrappers were then cut to a pattern from choice autumn-gold leaves. A white paste cemented the last layer of the wrapper. The ends then were carefully tapered. The damp cigars were placed in a damp mold to attain a uniform shape. Later they were packed in boxes of 50 cigars to a box. The last phase of the job, packing, was done by another group of girls who also had a quota to meet.

Even though Aunt Sadie was responsible for Bella she still had to make her quota each day. Workers averaged fifty hours a week with only a short half-hour break at noon for lunch.

Bella was always impressed with the lunches that Aunt Sadie had fixed for them, usually from the dinner of the night before. When lunch was over the whistle blew and everyone trudged back to their respective places at their table.

Bella worked ten hours a day, six days a week. For this she was paid one silver dollar! That was the wage for an apprentice. Bella later learned that Aunt Sadie could earn as much as eight dollars a week while some of the better shapers could earn as much as twelve or even fifteen! Bella convinced herself that she too would soon be earning fifteen dollars.

Bella learned that there was no discrimination between male and female workers. The "piece-price" plan was in effect. This meant that the more cigars one could shape the more money one could earn. However, many of the workers didn't like it if you went too fast. Bella remembered the day that she received an elbow in her side. The girl next to her at the table had poked her in the ribs saying, What the hell are you doing?" Bella responded by saying, "I'm going to get that bonus by rolling as many cigars as I can." The girl answered, "Don't you realize, you dummy, that if you roll more cigars they'll raise our quota?" When Bella spoke with Aunt Sadie about this Bella learned that it might be better if she slowed down a bit and just made her quota.

The end of the first few months had come rapidly. She couldn't believe how rapidly the time was flying by. Bella always looked forward to going up to the paymasters window and collecting her wages at the end of the week. She wanted to prove to Mama and Grandfather how much she had grown up and how important to the family she had become. Bella remembered the end of the first week that she had worked. Bella felt embarrassed and humiliated. The foreman told Bella that she could not go to the paymaster's window and pick up her pay. Even though it was just one silver dollar, Aunt Sadie had to receive her pay for her. It was then given to Mama. If Bella were lucky she would receive a few pennies for herself.

* * * * * *

It was on one of the Sunday afternoons when Bella was visiting at the Wescott's that Bella formally met Richard Woodruff. Bella had been playing the piano for a group of visitors when Richard came up to the piano and re-introduced himself. "I had instantly fallen in love with this dark-haired beauty playing the piano last July," he told her. He said he wanted to get to know her better.

GEORGE ROGER RICHARD LE PORTE

Richard was the son of Charles Woodruff who had a business relationship with George Westcott. It seemed that the manufacture of the vast quantity of cigars demanded corresponding production of cigar boxes. Some companies made their own boxes, but typical of the new industries arising out of the cigar making was the Charles Woodruff Company, begun in 1875.

Bella was thrilled to think that this very important guest would take any kind of interest at all in her. Richard told her that he was attending Hamilton College in Clinton, New York where he was a pre-law student although his major was in business. He was hoping, he said to one day go into business with his father. Richard began to tell her all about his father's factory. Bella was enthralled. Richard told her how his father had begun in 1875 to make boxes for the cigars that Mr. Westcott's factory turned out. He went on describing how, by 1890, the factory had grown to the point where they had hired thirty-four hands who turned out 700,000 boxes a year! Richard seemed proud of the fact that most of the workers were women. He pointed out that there was no discrimination made on the part of the Woodruff family.

Richard told Bella that his pre-law major in college was by design. He cited the fact that the growth of cigars could be readily seen in the annual number of cigars manufactured in Binghamton. In 1880, he pointed out; the number of cigars shipped from Binghamton amounted to 25,000,000. In three years that number had grown to 45,000,000 and by 1890 the number had risen to 120,000,000! This kind of growth calls for a lot of cigar boxes, Richard said. He and his father would be able to make other investments so that he would be looking at a secure future in the business. He also indicated that he was interested in dabbling in politics.

Richard was smitten the minute he had laid eyes on Bella. He asked her to go for a walk in the garden with him. They sat for hours it seemed, to Bella, as Richard told her all about college life and his plans for the future. Richard didn't seem to pry into Bella's background and she was too embarrassed to let him know anything at all about herself. When Richard leaned over and kissed her after telling her that he had fallen madly in love with her, Bella began to cry. Richard was dumbfounded. He sat quietly as Bella recounted to him their flight from Europe, their trip on the steamer coming to America, her going to school as a student of Miss Westcott and the piano lessons they most graciously had given to her. She left out the fact that she was already working at Mr. Westcott's cigar factory as a shaper of cigars. Despite this confession Richard iterated that he had to see her again. He was desperately in love with her. Bella knew all along, however, that the two of them came from different worlds. Even though Richard said she would be included in his summer plans Bella knew that it would be quite the contrary. She had heard all about summer vacations in the Finger Lakes from Agnes. There would be parties and dances. There would be swimming and tennis. The country club always had something going on for the adults and that gave the kids a lot of opportunity to have their own parties, usually on the beach with a bon-fire glowing in the night. Agnes also told her that the boys sometimes brought flasks of alcohol and there was much pairing off and smooching going on. "That was the most fun," Agnes said! Bella knew the reality was that she would be at work in the factory while all this was going on in Richard's life.

Bella didn't really get to see much of Richard during the summer that he was home from school because she still had to work in the factory and he had his friends with their camps in the Finger Lakes region of New York. It seemed to Bella that there was nothing but parties for Richard throughout the summer of their first meeting.

But, one day, while she was visiting at Miss Wescott's, Agnes popped in with some of her friends. There, too, was Richard much to Bella's surprise. When Richard spotted Bella he came over to her side and whispered that he truly had missed her despite the fact that he was away almost all of the summer. He went on to explain that his being away from her was more of a familial obligation than something that he had wanted. It was the expected thing to do since their families had been spending summers together since they were all little babies. Richard told Bella that he had his father's car and wanted Bella to go for a ride with him so that they could talk and make some plans about the future. Bella hesitated but Richard was so insistent that she agreed to slip away with him when the others had become distracted.

Richard and Bella headed west toward Elmira and the countryside of Big Flats. The two youngsters made idle talk about the things that they had done through the summer. Bella mostly listened since her life at the factory was not nearly as exciting as Richard's. His summer was full of dances, socials, fun at the beach and gatherings of the families of his parents' friends and he would soon be returning to his fraternity house, Delta Kappa Epsilon, at Hamilton College to complete his senior year. After that he would be looking for a good law school to get in to. Most probably it would be at Syracuse University – a good Methodist college that both of his grandfathers had attended.

Before long, Richard turned the car off the main road and was heading down a country lane. A place he said was quiet and where they could talk some more about their future. At the end of the road Bella spotted a beautiful apple tree alongside the Susquehanna river. The river was calm and without a ripple that afternoon. It was flowing so smoothly that it appeared to be like a looking glass. It was as blue as the sky but without the pretty white clouds from above. It was so very quiet when the motor was turned off. Richard told Bella that he had a blanket in the trunk of the car. He could put it out on the grass so that they could be more comfortable as they enjoyed the surrounding calm of the afternoon. Bella agreed. After some initial small talk Richard turned toward Bella and began to tell her that he thought of her constantly. Even when he went to the parties that summer with his friends, he told her, his mind was on her. No girl that he had met that summer could measure up to the beauty she had. He told her that he loved her.

Bella took a deep breath. Although she was flattered she reminded Richard of the two dramatically different backgrounds that they shared. Richard, she reminded him, was expected to marry the daughter of one of his parents' friends regardless of what he thought and she, Bella, was not in that class. Her background as an immigrant to this country and working in a factory did not sound like the kind of relationship Richard's parents had in mind for him.

Even though she sounded very convincing Richard leaned closer to her. He put his arm around her shoulders, pulled her toward him and kissed her warmly on the mouth. This was Bella's first kiss!

Even though it seemed the natural thing to do because even in spite of their differences she too thought she was in love with Richard.

Bella was not ready for what came next. Richard's strong athletic body was on top of her holding her wrists so that she couldn't move her arms. Richard's warm tongue opened her lips and with the tip of his tongue he ran it across the roof of her mouth. She began to feel a trembling that she had never experienced before. She cried out for him to stop but he went on. Richard had heard the plea to stop many times at the fraternity parties at the Deke House. The gentle "no" was expected, he thought, and kept on. With his left hand Richard began to unbutton the buttons of her blouse. Even though Bella had protested, Richard continued on his quest.

He had pushed her brassiere up over her breasts and began to suckle the rose-colored tips as they began to harden. Bella began experience feelings and sensations she had never felt before! Bella sat bolt upright when his hand touched her breast. She had never been this intimate with anyone before. No one, not even mama had seen her this way.

Richard kept on although Bella struggled fiercely. She was no match for him.. He whispered in her ear that he loved her. He told her how much she had meant to him. All this time his hands were in the process of disrobing her. First her blouse had come off, almost magically. Before she even knew what was happening her bra was off. Bella pushed away from Richard. She pleaded with him to stop. However, he insisted that this was the natural thing for both of them. After all, he said, he loved her and she loved him and besides no one would be coming down this road where they were parked. His mouth was all over her breasts. The tip of his tongue caressed the hardened pink nipples. Bella was still feeling things that she had never felt before. She was still fighting to get free from Richard's vise-like grip. His hand was under her dress and his fingers sought the edge of her panties. His fingers were now stroking her soft, silky, pubic hairs. All of a sudden she felt something warm "down there." This too, was a feeling she had never experienced nor felt before. Richard was pulling her panties off. She tried to protest but he was too strong for her. His body was on top of hers now and he was pulling down his pants and his under-shorts. Bella could not see what was happening to her. She could only feel the weight of his body on hers and the spreading of her legs by his seemingly educated fingers and hands. She felt the hardness of his manhood. All of a sudden there was a pain that made her cry out. He had put his manhood into her vagina. Bella began to cry but soon after she felt an electricity throughout her entire body that felt warm but the pain was still there. Richard ravished her and when it was over told Bella that he couldn't believe that she was a virgin. He knew that from his first penetration and then by the blood that was on the blanket. Bella began to cry.

She thought of Mama and Grandfather. What would they say? What would they do? She remembered stories from back in the village. The gossipers' stories, in bits and pieces, about girls who had gotten into trouble. She remembered the old ladies reminiscing over the olden days in the Torah that told of adulteresses and fornicators being stoned to death! Now she was one of them! Richard told her to get herself dressed. No one would ever know what had happened there, he told her, just the two of them.

When Bella had gotten herself dressed and the two of them were ready to go, Richard once again told her how much he loved her and that as soon as he finished college they could be married. He went on to tell her that he was truly looking forward to that day. Richard also told Bella that he would write to her every day. Bella panicked and told Richard she didn't think that would be such a good idea. If mail came to the house, Mama would get suspicious and start to wonder what was going on. The two of them held each other and kissed warmly once again, soon after Bella had calmed down. Richard started up the car and told Bella he wanted to get her home before it got dark.

* * * * * *

When Bella walked into the kitchen Mama was there, standing over the stove, getting their supper ready. She took one look at Bella and asked her what was the matter, Bella said there was nothing wrong and why did she ask. Mama said Bella had looked flushed. Mama added that she had hoped Bella was not coming down with anything. Bella told her mother that she just needed to freshen up before supper and went off to her room.

* * * * * *

In the weeks to come Bella tried to act, in front of the family, as if nothing was wrong. She continued to go to work at the factory with aunt Sadie. However, for weeks she agonized over what had happened. She felt guilty and somehow blamed herself. She felt that somehow she had encouraged Richard to do what he had done. The pain within her continued. She felt pain when she walked or even when she sat down. All this on top of the guilt she was feeling. She felt humiliated, soiled and somehow responsible for what had happened. As the days passed into weeks these negative thoughts kept building up and rolling around inside of her head increasing to a point of depression. She did her best to try to hide her feelings but always felt a deep-seated feeling of disgrace.

Mama was getting suspicious. She noticed by the increased number of times that Bella went to the bathroom. She listened at the doorway and could hear the discomfort that Bella was having whenever she would throw up. Although mama suspected she never said a word to Bella.

* * * * * *

Some months later the shaping room was a buzz of speculation. Everyone had been talking about a strike that was looming ahead.

The year 1890 is marked as the turning point in the history and the development of the cigar industry in Binghamton. This year was marked by labor unrest throughout the country as well as the world. The growth and development of labor unions, specifically the reorganization of the Knights of Labor in the form of the American Federation of Labor accounted for much of this. However, this did not just come about overnight.

The decades of the 1880's and 1890's were marked by all kinds of industrial conflict throughout the United States. From 1881 through 1886, three thousand nine hundred two strikes occurred involving twenty-two thousand three hundred establishments and one million three hundred twenty-three thousand men! This tempo was kept up for many years.

The chief reasons for the strikes included demands for increased wages, opposition to wage reductions and agitation for reduced hours of work.

These attitudes were reflected in the daily headlines of the Binghamton Democratic Weekly Leader that helped Binghamtonians learn that their plight was no different from anywhere else in the world. Grandfather and Uncle Louis pondered over the headlines each morning before going off to work.

Some of the headlines, as early as 1890 read as follows:

Friday, March 28, 1890

CHICAGO CIGARMAKERS UNION #4 CALLS FOR GENERAL STRIKE OVER WAGES

Friday, April 25, 1890

SHORTER HOURS AND INCREASED PAY STRIKES; MILWAUKEE, BUFFALO, QUINCY, MASS. NEWBURGH, CHICAGO, ST. LOUIS AND PHILADELPHIA

BELLA

Friday, May 2, 1890

8-HOUR MOVEMENT – DATELINE NEW YORK; CHICAGO, MILWAUKEE ELIZABETH, NEW JERSEY, AND BOSTON

Grandfather and Uncle Louis would sit down after the evening supper and discuss the conditions at their own cigar factory with Aunt Sadie. Bella was always too tired to enter into these discussions and would excuse herself in order to lie down in her room.

Aunt Sadie told Uncle Louis and grandfather they had heard that there were efforts on the part of the Cigarmaker's International, an affiliate of the newly created American Federation of Labor, to organize the cigar workers of Binghamton. A general industry-wide strike was to be called for on June 25th, 1890.

It was determined that this strike would not fail, folks said, as had been the case in the previous year when during the winter of 1889 when there was an abortive strike.

"Workers were forced to submit to the manufacturers. Wages were reduced by five cents, from thirty cents, on a hundred cigars. Quotas were instituted and the workers were compelled to cut their wrappers closer in order to prevent waste. This necessitated slower work," Aunt Sadie said, "and reduced the earnings of the workers even more since they were working on a piece rate."

Aunt Sadie reported that one of the committeemen for the strikers remarked, just that morning, "It is war. War to the knife, and lots of knife if the manufacturers won't give in."

The strikers declared that they would stick together, and that this time they had the support of the Cigar-maker's International, the Knights of Labor and the Farmer's Alliance. Rumor had it that twenty-five thousand dollars would be sent from New York alone to help the strikers, if necessary.

* * * * * * *

As the days went on there was much secrecy and silence on the part of the strikers as to what their plans and proposals might be. This silence and secrecy was interpreted by management as meaning a lack of confidence in the power that the strikers might have in seeing this through to success. Therefore, they did not anticipate a long strike.

The initial discontent of the workers over wages was met with the statement from the managements of the various cigar factories that business would not warrant any increases. Since competition would not warrant wage increases the prospect of a prolonged strike would only hurt the Binghamton cigar industry!

The attitude of all the manufacturers can best be reflected in the statement issued by the manufacturer's association for the Broome County Republican newspaper, "We will move our factories and all our possessions and interests to some other city if we cannot get workmen here."

This was followed by a letter to the Editor of The Democratic Weekly Leader that outlined the positive attitude and demands of the workers:

BELLA

"To the Editors,

Will you kindly give space in your paper for the following statement from the striking cigarmakers? This strike, which no business man deplores more heartily than do the cigar-makers, has been forced on the workmen. Since the last general strike in this city, the cigar-makers have been subjected to several direct cuts in prices, and to reductions indirectly by the introduction of the more difficult shapes of cigars, as well as by a rule that requires a greater number of cigars to be made from a pound of fillers and wrappers, thus making the workman slower and reducing his earnings.

And while wages have been gradually decreasing, until the average wages do not exceed one dollar a day, the prices of the necessaries of life have gradually increased until cigar-makers have been obliged to send their wives and children into the shops. At the same time many instances may be mentioned of manufacturers who started on borrowed capital ten years ago and are now living in palaces, driving fast horses, and sporting diamonds.

To no thinking person will it be necessary to brand as utterly untrue, the statement that Binghamton cigar firms cannot compete with those of New York City. These manufacturers could easily pay twice or three times the present prices and still undersell New York City in any market in the country, for the single reason that in New York City manufacturers must pay excessive rents, while Binghamton manufacturers own their own shops and pay nothing but taxes.

Prices paid by the firms in New York

And Binghamton are here given and comment is unnecessary:

ROLLING

Length of Cigars	New York	Binghamton
4"	$ 4.90	$ 2.50
4 ¼"	5.10	2.50
4 ½"	5.30	2.50
4 ¾ - 5"	5.45	2.50

BUNCHES

Length of Cigars	New York	Binghamton
4"	$ 2.00	1.20
4 ¼"	2.10	1.20
4 ½"	2.20	1.20
4 ¾"	2.25	1.20
5"	2.30	1.20

SHAPER TEAM WORK

Length of Cigars	New York	Binghamton
4"	9.30	5.50 – 6.50
4 ¼"	10.00	7.00
4 ½"	10.70	7.00
4 ¾ - 5"	11.60	7.00 – 8.00

(This price list is complete) With the exception, probably not to exceed half a dozen jobs, where they pay a little more than the above prices.

The strikers request the public not to accept as authoritative anything, which does not bear the signature of the printing committee.

/s/ M. Kelley
John J. Doyle
John A. Cecil
Edward F. Dunn
Committee on Printing

The manufacturers were almost unanimous in declaring that they could not afford to pay the increase in prices demanded. They maintained that competition, especially in New York City and Pennsylvania, "is too warm for them."

They took the position that during the dull season (summer) they kept their factories going merely for the purpose of giving their hands employment, and that now they had an immense stock on hand.

Immediately after this announcement some two thousand rollers and bunch-makers left their tables and met at Leonard's hall to discuss the wage situation.

The meeting was called to order at eight p.m. by S.P. Gorman of the Reynolds, Rogers & Company's Cigar Factory, who acted as Chairman. Thomas Sweeney, of the Rossville factory, was Secretary. The purpose of the meeting, as announced by Mr. Sweeney, was to get an increase of pay of five cents on a hundred for rolling cigars. Rollers, he pointed out, were now receiving twenty-five cents a hundred at the present rate.

GEORGE ROGER RICHARD LE PORTE

Spokesmen for the bunch-making branch of the industry, which was almost exclusively made up of women, spoke of their dissatisfaction, too. Aunt Sadie sat quietly with Bella next to her. They were obligated to attend the meeting for fear that their co-workers might ostracize them if they were noticeably absent from the scene. The spokesperson went on to say that a uniform price of twelve cents was being paid to bunch-makers. A price increase of three cents a hundred was decided upon for them.

It was also decided that only a strike of all cigar-makers in the city would succeed, and therefore, plans were made to induce other workmen to join the strikers unless the increase was acceded to.

* * * * * *

Aunt Sadie and Bella were quick to get home with the news for Uncle Louis and Grandfather and Mama to share. They agreed that they surely needed the advice of all inasmuch as it would affect all of the family!

On the way home Aunt Sadie asked Bella to look into her eyes. She told Bella that she had an idea of what was happening to her and asked if she couldn't confide in her. After all, Aunt Sadie said, I had two children. I would be stupid if I didn't know what the signs of pregnancy were. Bella burst into tears. She blurted out the entire story of how she had met Richard months ago at a soiree that Mrs. Westcott had put on for her friends. She went on to say that after summer vacation was almost over she bumped into Richard again. He had asked her to go for a ride in his father's automobile. And, since she had never been in such an elegant machine she had accepted. They drove into the country, Bella went on, and there, Richard had professed his abounding love for her.

At this point Aunt Sadie interrupted and said, "Ketzile, they all tell you that they're madly in love with you – until they get into your pants!" "You should have known better. Certainly you must have heard stories going around the factory from girls who have had similar experiences. Didn't you listen?"

"Does your Mama and grandfather know yet?" Bella responded in the negative but added, "I think Mama knows." "Then we must tell her," Aunt Sadie said. You have no idea what a burden you are going to put your mama and family through.

It was late when they arrived at Bella's home. Uncle Louis was waiting there, too. They couldn't wait to hear the news. "Sooo," said Uncle Louis. Aunt Sadie took the lead. She told everyone exactly what had happened and added that they were in a predicament. They did not want to be known as scabs, yet they needed the income from working. Aunt Sadie added that they were also fearful of losing their jobs if the strike ended badly and the factory owners decided to fire all of the workers who went out on strike. Uncle Louis didn't think that that would happen. "After all," he said, "where would they find the workers who were already trained to do what you do?" "The worst that could happen," he added, "would be that they cut your wages. If that should happen, we'll just have to learn to live with a little less. Remember, we have a little saved. We can get by for a time. Now let's have some coffee and strudel that my talented niece made."

"Before we do that," Aunt Sadie said, "we have more news for everyone. Go ahead, Bella. Tell them."

Bella burst into tears and retold the story that she had told Aunt Sadie on the on the way home.

Mama's first reaction was to tell Bella what a stupid thing she had done. "Do you realize what you have done? We are struggling as it is. And now, this." I have a good mind to throw you out into the street where all girls like you should be." "I'll bet it was you who led this boy on. What were you thinking? Did you think that he would all of a sudden whisk you off your feet and carry you home to his hoity-toity family and they would welcome you into their fold with open arms?"

At this point Aunt Sadie intervened. She told Mama that she was right to be upset. However, she explained, it wasn't Bella's encouragement so much as her naivety that made all of this happen. "Even so," Aunt Sadie went on "we are family and we must work this out together."

Mama hugged her daughter with tears in her eyes and assured her child that they would see this through and work it out. "Does the boy know?" Mama wanted to know. Bella replied, "No." "Then he shall never know," declared Mama. We will raise him according to our faith. He will have lots of love."

"Why do you say him, Mama?" Mama replied, "I can tell the way you are carrying your child that it will be a boy."

Bella was frightened when her water broke, Mama sent Grampa to fetch the midwife. The pain was awful. Bella was in tears and in dreadful pain. When the midwife arrived she calmed everyone down including Bella. As she managed to get Bella to relax and get into a rhythm of pushing and breathing it happened. Sure enough when the child came it was a boy. But, he was unlike the children of her ancestry. This child was born with yellow hair, not black, And, his eyes were blue not brown. Bella took the bundle from the hands of the midwife and peered into his face. She was overwhelmed with her accomplishment. He was a beautiful baby. Even mama had to agree that this child was something special. Aunt Sadie had been summoned too when the news from Grampa came that the time had arrived. Aunt Sadie looked at the happy face of Bella and cooed along with Mama. They both knew that this child was special.

Bella wanted to name him Richard after his father but the family, who declared that a good Biblical name like David would be much more appropriate, overruled her. "It's a good strong name, Mamma said, that goes back to the house of Abraham." So it was done. The rabbi conducted the bris and David, who was a healthy chubby baby, would know lots of love as he grew up especially from Miss Westcott, who was there and proclaimed herself David's godmother.

* * * * * *

In the meantime the strike went on. The workers formed their picket lines just outside of the factories where they worked. They were joined with members of their families who had already set up makeshift quarters by using tents. Inside the tent there was always a coffee pot steaming while the women chatted and made sandwiches for the brave men who marched along the picket line with their signs that declared the unfair labor practices of their employers. The police were there watching the proceedings.

It was a peaceful scene until about ten o'clock one day when, for no apparent reason, the police got into their cruiser and drove away. At about the same time three large black REO touring cars pulled up about one hundred feet away. The men in the cars got out of them carrying a baseball bat in one hand and chains in the other. Without warning they attacked the picketers and their families. Baseball bats swung at the shins of the picketers. The picketers fell to the ground in excruciating pain. While on the ground squirming and screaming the baseball bats found their way all over the bodies of the picketers. These goons made no distinction between men or women; they just pummeled away swearing invectives at the helpless people. One of the women had her dress torn off her body! She leaned back against the factory fence covering her bare breasts with her cupped hands and held her knees together in an effort to hide her privates. She was sobbing. One of the men was grabbed by two of the goons. He was pushed face down onto the pile of coals that were in the barrel heating the coffee. His screams of pain were deafening. The smell of the burning skin was horrific while still others were brutally pummeled. Signs were torn and broken into many pieces. It didn't take long for the place to have looked like Armageddon! They would have continued with their beatings had it not been for the sirens of the police cars approaching from a short distance away. The goons scrambled back into their cars and drove away. They were completely gone by the time the police had arrived. The chief himself was among the police at the site. The chief demanded to know what was going on. When the spokesperson for the picketers tried to explain the chief responded by saying, "That's a likely story." "You must have been fighting amongst yourselves." When he saw the nude woman lying next to the fence he said to the strikers, "Now I know what the fight was all about. Things must have gotten dull here." He never waited for anyone's explanations. "Anyway," he went on to say, "You folks have no right to be here. You're disturbing the peace and you have no permit to assemble outside this shop. I'm arresting you. Come with me down to the police station." The police carted off several of the men and women in their patrol cars.

It was early in July that Samuel Gompers came to Binghamton to give encouragement to the strikers and to urge them to stick together. He gave two speeches.

In the first speech, after being introduced as the President of the American Federation of Trades, he began by reminding the strikers that there was turmoil all over the world.

"Labor is rising and shaking his shackles and chains. Labor is moving. It is in accordance with a natural law arising from a natural condition, and just as water will run downhill, although the ingenuity of man sometimes forces it uphill; just as the sun shines, although we have roofs, umbrellas, and parasols to divert its rays; just as the lightnings flash, although we have the lightning fork to divert it, so will labor go on breaking his chains in spite of efforts to restrain and divide his power, until at last he will stand up in the sunlight a free man. The time was when a man who talked of a labor question was considered an enemy of society, and supposed to be a creature whose hair stood out straight, whose hands and feet were claws and hoofs, from whose mouth issued flames and sulpher and brimstone. But today everyone is considering the labor question. It was the labor question that drove Bismarck, the man of 'Blood and Iron,' from power. The Emperor of Germany is considering the labor question. That grand old man of England is considering the labor question. In the United States, from the President down to the lowest officer, everyone is thinking of the labor question. You can measure a man's condition by what he wants. Go out into the streets and ask the man who has no home, no place to go, no one to care for him, the outcast, what he wants, and if he don't tell you he wants a drink he will tell you that he wants a good square meal. Ask the laborer who gets $1.00 a day and he will probably say that he wants five cents or ten cents more. Ask the man who gets $3.00 and he wants a quarter more. Ask the man who gets $5.00 and he wants a dollar more.

Ask the man who gets $5,000 and he wants $6,000, ask the man who has $500,000 and he wants $500,000 more to make it $1,000,000. Everybody wants more. I am glad that Binghamton's cigarmakers have decided not to be slaves any longer. It seemed too good to be true, that at last the cigar makers of Binghamton have awakened from the sleep; they have at last come out of the cloud that had enveloped them so long; they have cast off the incubus that has pressed upon their breasts; you have at last asserted that you are men and women."

At this point there was a loud and raucous cheer from the workmen seated in the hall. Up to this point, Aunt Sadie had noticed, they were clinging to Mr. Gompers' every word in complete silence. But here was something to cheer about and they did.

Mr. Gompers went on after the din had faded away. "This strike should convince you that the bosses do not care about you because you are from Binghamton; if they could get Elmira girls and boys to fill your places, they will employ them; if they could get African men and women, they would hire them; they would employ monkeys if they could get them. The only objection they would have to monkeys would be they would have to hire two men to watch one monkey."

Another roar was heard along with laughter from most of the workers.

Mr. Gompers went on by stating that he had been a cigarmaker for twenty-five years of the forty years of his life, and he had been in a number of strikes, so many that he had forgotten the number. He stated that he had always been slow to go on strike. He did not believe in rushing up in the shop and shouting, "Strike." He said he believed in holding meetings to discuss the matter, and if a majority were in favor of strike, he went out – whether he approved it or not – to stay out until the bosses gave in to their demands, or he never went back.

He asked the workers to suppose that all the firms had gone out of business; suppose all the bosses were to "blow up;" suppose they were to "explode or dry up," or suppose that by some peculiar set of circumstances, "they were all to die at once." What would you do the? You would make no more cigars in Binghamton, would you? You must suppose them all dead until they sign your bill of prices."

He gave it as his opinion that the Chief of Police had exceeded his authority in ordering the pickets to discontinue their vigilance. He said that he would consult with the Attorney General of the State, and he would find that they were justified in the course of action they were pursuing.

Mr. Gompers said he would picket a shop himself in the morning. He urged them the necessity of organization, and of having the whole United States and Canada behind them.

He reminded them that one of the reasons these manufacturers had opposed this paltry advance of five cents was that they feared that if the cigarmakers won this strike they would organize, and that would be a terrible thing for the bosses. If they lost the strike, they would place themselves entirely in the power of the manufacturer, and their condition would be worse than it ever was before.

"In every place there are people who smile when the boss smiles, who put on a long face when the boss has a toothache, who think always just as the boss does—the shop sucker. I do not know if you have such people here, but I have seen them everywhere I have been. Napoleon said,' I like the information, I like the treachery, but I hate the informer, and I despise the traitor.' So it is with the bosses; they may like to have the work done; they may like to have the shop sucker stay in the shop, but he hates a scab as much as you or I, and he will take the first opportunity to let those people go."

He concluded by hoping that they would continue to act as they had heretofore during the strike, peaceably and honestly.

He urged the pickets to be on duty, and to use every peaceable means possible to keep the shops empty.

Aunt Sadie joined in with the other workers who were cheering triumphantly as if they had already won the strike. Mr. Gompers had given them great hope and encouragement. However, it had been a long day and Aunt Sadie trudged home looking forward to climbing into a warm bed and getting a good night's sleep.

The next morning, Uncle Louis was sitting at the kitchen table reading to Aunt Sadie as she was making the coffee. From "The Democratic Weekly Leader." Mr. Gompers, he read, was described "as a man of striking personal appearance, of medium height and extremely dark complexion." The statement described him further, "he speaks in a clear, deliberate, forcible manner, with a very slight German accent."

As Uncle Louis was about to leave for work he reminded Aunt Sadie to be careful. If those goons come back again find a place to hide. There is no need for you to wind up in the hospital.

That morning, at 8 a.m., Mr. Gompers walked the picket line with a group of strikers in front of the Hull-Grummond Company. Aunt Sadie had been assigned to that group for the day and she felt especially proud to have been in the company of such a great man. Things went well. No one expected that anyone might interfere with Mr. Gompers inasmuch as he was an important and well-known man throughout the state, especially among politicians and within the labor movement.

Aunt Sadie announced that, after supper, she had to attend

another meeting of the workers in Leonard's Hall that evening. Mr. Gompers was to deliver another speech. She was eager to hear what this man had to say, especially after last night and today's march on the picket line with him.

The striking cigarmakers again assembled in large numbers in Leonard's hall to listen to the closing address of Mr. Samuel Gompers. After congratulating them on the interest they displayed in spite of the intense heat, he said:

"When any difficulty of this kind arose between employer and employed, when any strike occurred, it usually happened that the employers tried to cause dissension among the strikers—tried to divide the ranks. It seemed that very frequently when a man became a foreman into a cigar shop, he entered into a contract, as a scab-hunter, and sacrificed his liberty, his birthright, his honor, his manhood. The international union was right, knowing the kind of men foremen usually are, to say that no foreman, under any circumstances, shall become a member of the union. These men try to disunite the workmen by casting discredit upon their leaders. They say to this one or that one, 'Do you suppose for an instant that your President or your Secretary or your Strike Committee care whether you win this a strike or not? Don't believe any scandal concerning an officer. Any reports heard could be borne in mind until the trouble is over and then investigated, but most of these reports are out in circulation to create discord. Take Abe Lincoln's advice, 'Never swap horses when crossing a stream, you might get wet.' Don't accept the prices on a few jobs and let a few men go to work, leaving a majority of the men out. It is a trick of the bosses to get a few in their shops and then spread the report that the men are coming back again.

This strike of yours is but one of the incidents in the struggle of the human family for progress. We have seen the time men owned slaves. They didn't own slaves because they liked the slaves; they owned them because they owned their labor. All they care about you is to get your labor. The slave in the South was better off than the poorly paid workingman of today. The slave owner must give his slaves food and clothing, to keep him in good physical condition, get him medicine when he is sick, for if he died the owner was at a loss; but the bosses of today care more for their horses than for their workmen. They provide good food and well-ventilated houses for their horses. If a horse is sick they take good care of him, for if it dies, they will lose, while it matters not if the workers have poor food, or the factories are foul and ill-ventilated, and if the workers are sick or if they die, it matters not to them. And why should they care? They can get plenty of others.

When a manufacturer reckons on the cost of his goods, he counts so much for tobacco, so much for machines, so much for boxes, so much for labor. They value us as they do a block of wood or a machine. A manufacturer in Massachusetts said not long ago, 'I regard my workmen as so many machines. When they get old and rusty I throw them out in the street.' He had the courage to say it; the others think it.

The wages question involves more than is just supposed. The step below which we should not go is a fair living for every man or woman. We should try to eliminate from society the class who try to become rich without regard to the means. It seems most wicked to see men trying to get rich on the blood and sinew of little children. We are the people—that is, we are just before election. And we are then, and about the Fourth of July, supposed to have some rights such as 'life, liberty and the pursuit of happiness.'

We generally are in pursuit of happiness and usually reach unhappiness. Happiness is usually the thing which is ahead and it usually keeps ahead. Men and women in this country have some duties to perform. Men and women in America are supposed to be the equals of all. You are supposed to be the equal of the President; you are supposed to be the equal of the senators; you are supposed to be the equal of the Governor of your state; you are supposed to be the equal of the Lieutenant-Governor; you are supposed to be as good as anybody; but you are only supposed to be. You are supposed to cast your votes for the officers of this government; very often you cast so many ballots for your employer. A man who receives small wages is apt to have a poor opinion of his duty to the government. Men who receive small wages are more dependent upon the bosses. Frequently the boss will come into the factory just before election and say, 'I should like to see such and such a ticket elected;' or, 'It would be to the interest of the firm and to all connected to have so and so elected.' And woe to him who is caught voting any other way. A great deal is said in connection with the labor question about taxes. When taxes are high rents are high, the merchant adds to the price of his goods and provisions are dear. And you will find that every addition to taxes is paid by the workman.

Long ago, in Colonial times, there was an inn which had a sign board, and this sign illustrates exactly the position of the workmen, in the past and in the present. There were four figures. On the ground was a workman, upon his shoulders was a priest, upon the priest's shoulders was a king, upon the king's shoulders was a soldier.

From the mouth of each issued a motto.

The soldier said, 'I fight for all;' the king said, 'I rule all;' the priest said, 'I pray for all;' the workman said, 'I pay for all.'

Mr. Gompers concluded his address by urging the strikers to stand together, to keep their column unbroken and to remember that the weaker the other side got, the bolder a front they would put on.

The room went wild. The workers were greatly rejuvenated. They all pledged that they would not falter. They rushed to the podium to shake hands with this giant in the labor movement who had taken the time from his very busy and important schedule to care about them.

* * * * * *

Ironically, in the same column of the Democrat weekly Leader, immediately following Mr. Gompers' speech was the following advertisement:

LEARN A TRADE

YOUNG MEN AND WOMEN ARE WANTED TO LEARN THE CIGAR TRADE IN BINGHAMTRON, NEW YORK. FOR FULL PARTICULARS READ THE ADVERTISEMENT IN ANOTHER COLUMN AND

GEORGE ROGER RICHARD LE PORTE

ADDRESS INQUIRIES TO THE REYNOLDS TOBACCO COMPANY, BINGHAMTON, New York.

* * * * * *

In the meantime, Bella was learning to cope with motherhood. She was very fortunate. Mama just adored little David. You'd think it was her own. She instructed Bella when it came to breast-feeding and changing diapers. Mama would sit in her rocking-chair after coming home from cleaning the homes of the well-to-do and sing songs that she had remembered from her childhood while young David was thriving on their love. He was a happy baby.

It was also time for Bella to report back to work. The family could use the money that she earned. However, she was in a quandary. Aunt Sadie had warned her not to go back because she would be considered a scab and would be despised by her co-workers if she did. She didn't know what to do until one Saturday Miss. Wescott came up with an answer. Miss Westcott never missed a Saturday. She brought story books and would read to David seemingly for hours at a time. By four years of age David was reading aloud with her.

Miss Westcott told Bella and Mama that she was worried, too. She didn't feel that Bella should go back to the factory floor to work, especially with the turmoil still continuing, She, too, was worried that Bella might get hurt. Mama agreed, but what was the answer? Mama said, "You've been so kind to us for so long and here you are looking out for us again. Mama settled down into a chair across from Miss Westcott and asked what did she have in mind? Mama added, "the real problem is to find a suitable job for Bella. With all of the problems of the strike going on it is rather dangerous for Bella, in her condition, to return to the factory job as a shaper."

Miss Westcott agreed with Mama. She added that she would talk to her father about putting Bella into the office. Bella is bright. She can learn fast and has the ability to do well in an office job. Miss. Westcott was certain, she told mama, that she could arrange things very soon.

Two days later Miss Westcott kept her promise. She had arranged for Bella to start in the office as a clerk. Miss Hazel Ives, the head bookkeeper and right hand to Mr. Westcott would train Bella.

* * * * * *

The strike went on. The employers stood firm in their position of not wanting to meet the demands of the strikers. But too, they made it perfectly clear that they objected to meeting with any representatives of the Cigarmakers International Union. The factory owners regarded them as instigators and agitators.

In the early stages of the strike, the Manufacturers' Association brought workers to Binghamton from Pennsylvania at a rate of fifty dollars a day.

This was followed by wholesale recruitment of people to be employed in the factories at standard wages.

These workmen, imported from the York and Lancaster regions of Pennsylvania were required to sign a contract that bound them to work at the present wage scale for a period of one year.

Young boys and girls were also recruited from nearby Elmira.

"Don't be afraid," said George Mc Guire, Union Organizer. "These men from Pennsylvania are brought here primarily to show that they, the manufacturers, have men in the shops. They do not know how to cut Sumatra stock. It is not used in the cheap districts."

At this time the cigarmakers of Binghamton were not yet organized, even though a convention of the Cigarmakers' International was held in Binghamton two years prior, in 1888.

Hundreds of cigarmakers from all parts of the country were present at that convention and the proceedings were conducted harmoniously and successfully.

P.J. Mc Guire told them, "The cigarmakers were originally organized to break up the truck system of paying off men. Under this system the men were given an order on some merchant to whom the manufacturer sold cigars, or they were paid in cigars, which they turned over to the storekeepers in exchange for supplies. The workmen received no money!"

At the convention, the cigarmakers of Binghamton were asked to join the union. The answer from the cigarmakers was, "No."

They cited the fact that there never had been any serious labor difficulties in Binghamton and their relationship with their employers had always been good.

Ironically, a few weeks after this refusal there was a cut in wages of all cigarmakers working on Sumatra stock. The cut represented a two-thirds decrease in average wages and was made without the consultation of the cigarmakers.

Frank Haller of New York City, who at the time was President of the New York branch of the American Federation of Labor and an organizer for the Cigarmakers International said, "The reduction of wages of the working people of Binghamton is injurious not only to the workingmen themselves, but to the business people as well. Owing to this last cut in wages the employees of the cigar shops of this city will have from thirty to forty thousand dollars less to spend per year with your various business houses, and the consumer of cigars is not benefited for a five cent cigar will continue to be sold for five cents whether the dealer buys it for a dollar less a thousand. Nor will the Binghamton manufacturers be able to profit long by the reduction in wages. The jobbers and the retailers will press them with that unrestrainable pressure, competition, until they are compelled to relinquish that which they have taken from their employees. The cut in the wages of the Binghamton rollers and bunchmakers is a cut down of the local interests for the benefit of the retailers in the West and Southwest where Binghamton cigars are sold."

* * * * * *

The employers were optimistic that the strike would not last long. Their attitude was reflected by Mr. Charles Hull of Hull and Grummond was that they were just young people letting off steam and enjoying a summer vacation.

On the other hand, the very same Mr. Hull was responsible

for bringing about conspiracy charges against the various people who were on picket duty in front of his establishment.

It is noteworthy to mention that the influence of religion on the strikers was not left untapped. The manufacturers in an effort to put pressure on families recruited Father Brennan, of Saint Mary's Roman Catholic Church to give a talk to the ladies and girls in an effort to end the strike.

By July 22nd only one small plant had signed a contract meeting the strikers' demands after the firm of Carter and Darrow went bankrupt on July 16th as a result of the strike.

The F.R. Keyes and Company bankruptcy followed the next day. Mr. Keyes stated, "the bankruptcy was the result of the strike of the cigarmakers and the failure of creditors and customers to accommodate them through the enforced idleness of the factory. "

At the beginning of the strike, the company did not have any manufactured goods on hand in stock. They could not fill orders for goods thereby losing five hundred dollars a day.

Mr. Henry Schubmehl operated the plant that signed a contract. The plant employed fifty to sixty hands.

The Manufacturers' Association did not consider this to be a threat to their position but it did give some temporary hope to the strikers.

On the 25th of July the strikers were able to bring Ralph Strasser, President of the American Federation of Labor, to Binghamton. He told the strikers:

"You are receiving less than half the wages paid in other

parts of the country. You are receiving less that is paid the Chinese working at the trade in California. Their cheapest work is five dollars per thousand while you are making three dollars and seventy cents! Wherever you go you hear that Binghamton cigars are sold for less than the cigars from any other city.

I would like to call your attention to the prices paid in the city of Westfield it comes in close competition with Binghamton. They have been receiving for scrap bunches two dollars and fifty cents, for rolling dry work four dollars and fifteen cents, for rolling shapers four dollars and sixty-five cents and they are now asking to go on strike to advance rolling dry work to four dollars and sixty-five cents, shapes four dollars and eighty-five cents. The cheapest job in St. Louis is nine dollars and yet your manufacturers have the cheek to say they cannot compete with them. I believe that if Binghamton manufacturers are champions in anything, they are champions in lying. They say that the strikers are breaking the law. The manufacturers have been breaking the laws every day. There is a law on the state books which says that children shall not be employed under fourteen years, yet they are defying and breaking the law every day.

They have been appealing to the police commissioners to make laws to compel the pickets to desist. A decision has been rendered by Judge Macomber of Buffalo and by several other courts and they have decided that picketing is lawful.

If you win tomorrow and do not join a union they will soon take away all they have given. If you have the union back of you, you will in case of trouble, have ten thousand dollars a week pouring into this city to support you. The funds of the International Union are two hundred eighty-five thousand dollars."

The attitude of the manufacturers remained the same. The words of George A. Kent typified their feelings.

"As to the present struggle, it is, I believe, brought about by the international Cigarmakers' Union, which has wanted its twenty-five cents a week out of our workmen here for a long time. There are thousands of them and the aggregate would be large. This union has agitators here, and had them here when the strike began. It was started by them, and they gain. The people are dupes, and I am sorry for them."

"As for the manufacturers giving in, I don't think they can or will—that is George A. Kent and Company. We cannot and will not. I will close my factory forever before I will submit to any dictation on the part of any union."

Early in August, Mr. F. F. Donovan of the New York State Board of Arbitration made his appearance on the scene. He called for a meeting to be held between the strikers and the manufacturers in the Supervisor's Room at the Court House.

Mr. Donovan opened the session with a few remarks in which he called attention to the supreme necessity of settling the strike controversy, both in the interests of the parties involved and those of the community.

Mr. Curtiss, a Senior Counsel for the strikers submitted their proposal to the board. It covered the following points:

FIRST, we are not willing to settle this controversy upon the basis of allowing the manufacturers of the city of

Binghamton a profit of more than eight per cent of the gross sales. In addition to allowing each member of the firm and each individual engaged in the manufacture of cigars—on each sale made by him—the same compensation that is paid employees for similar services, and each member of a firm and each individual who performs services in the business, whether a foreman, manager, agent, etc., the same compensation that is paid for similar services.

SECOND, for the reason that in every class of business the basis for estimating profits is on the capital invested in the business and not on the gross sales or the amount of business done. It is well known that it requires but a small capital, comparatively speaking, to carry on this industry and a large volume of business can be done on a small amount of capital'

Again, the sales in this business are made either for cash or on ninety days time. If goods are sold on cash, eight per cent profit on such sales can be made as often as the cigars can be produced and converted into money. If the sales are made on ninety days time, the same capital can be turned over four times in one year, which is equivalent to a profit of eighty-two percent over and above the payment of all expenses and allowing salaries to the members of the firms and all parties in the business.

Again, the great mass of cigars made in Binghamton are sold for twenty-five dollars per thousand, which would be a profit of two hundred ten thousand dollars on one hundred five million cigars that were made in Binghamton last year, and this would be divided among the manufacturers in addition to the profits which they would make by being allowed the salaries and compensations for their individual services in their own business.

We submit that a statement upon this basis would be unjust, and does not touch the question of wages, which is the real question involved in this controversy. It cannot be urged that lower wages than are paid in other competing points must be accepted in order that capital may be so rewarded.

The cigarmakers in the city of Binghamton are insisting upon an advance in wages, being satisfied from their own knowledge of the prices which are being paid for the same class of work in other cities, that such advance can be paid by the manufacturers and still leave them ample profit, and at the same time give them a sufficient margin for the trade of the country.

Up to January 1st, 1889, the following prices were paid in this city: one dollar and twenty cents per thousand for buchmaking and three dollars per thousand for rolling. At this time all of the manufacturers but one reduced the price for rolling by five cents per hundred or fifty cents per thousand. This cut took at least fifty-two thousand dollars out of the labor of Binghamton and distributed it among retail dealers throughout the country. It caused a reduction in the price to jobbers but the retail dealers sold the cigars at the same price as they did before. A five-cent cigar is a five-cent cigar with them and it matters not what they pay for it.

For over a year and five months the employees protested against this reduction and demanded a restoration of prices. The Manufacturer's Association persistently refused to confer with them on the subject, and every demand that was made was received with a stern rebuke, if not with an insult, and after this long time of earnest petitioning, a resolve was made to try the last resort of a laboring man, to organize for self-protection and refuse to work. We were forced into this position. While we regret to leave our employers and our places in their factories under these circumstances, yet we did it only in response to a duty that we felt we owed to our families and ourselves.

Before going out on this strike we demanded the following increase in wages: three cents per hundred on scrap bunchmaking, two and one half cents per hundred on long filler and seed bunches, and five cents per hundred on long filler Havana bunches; and also that the price of shaper—which is an imitation of hand work—be made uniform.

Thus, we are now asking that the manufacturers of Binghamton pay us four dollars and fifty cents per thousand for making the lowest grade of cigars, or scrap work, for which we have formerly been paid three dollars and seventy cents per thousand.

The price paid in the City of New York for this same class of work is six dollars and sixty cents per thousand, and in other cities as follows: Albany, seven dollars; Syracuse $8.00; Utica seven dollars and fifty cents; Rochester eight dollars; Buffalo eight dollars; Westfield, Massachusetts, six dollars and fifty cents; Philadelphia, four dollars and fifty cents in which city the workmen are now on strike demanding more.

The grade of prices which we are demanding are much

lower than are paid in any other city for the same class of goods and we are unable to understand how it is that when taxes, insurance and rent are lower in Binghamton than in the larger cities, while the facilities for transportation are as good her as anywhere, that the manufacturers cannot compete and hold the trade and pay smaller wages than anywhere else.

THEREFORE, we respectfully submit on behalf of the employees the following proposition:

FIRST, The employees who are now on strike shall resume work in their respective factories in the city of Binghamton on Monday the 4th day of August, 1890;

SECOND, that the State Board of Arbitration shall immediately proceed to form themselves into a legal body and issue subpoenas to compel the attendance of witnesses, and to take evidence upon the price paid to labor for making the different shapes and grades of cigars which are manufactured heretofore and during the past year have been manufactured by the concerns whose employees are now on strike. This shall not include what is known as hand-made work, and the said Board of Arbitration shall also take evidence for the purpose of determining the prices paid for the same classes of cigars in other cities which come into competition in the markets of the country with cigars manufactured in this city, but such investigation shall not include the ninth district of the State of Pennsylvania, and if after hearing such evidence and making such investigation, the State Board of Arbitration shall determine that other cities and places that come into competition with this city in this industry are paying higher wages than the wages demanded by the cigarmakers of the

BELLA

City of Binghamton the following scale of prices to wit:

BILL OF PRICES

<u>4" or over</u> <u>Price demanded</u>	<u>Old Price</u>
Bunchmaking scrap	
$1.50	$1.20
Long filler Havana	
$3.00	$2.50
Rolling long filler	
$3.00	$2.50
Long filler seed	
$3.25	$2.50
Rolling scrap	
$3.00	$2.50
Rolling Havana	
$3.00	$2.50

<u>Shapes 4" or over per 1000</u>	
4" or over mixed seed	
$6.00	$7.00
Re-rolled seed	
$6.00	$7.50
4" or over Havana	
$8.00	$9.50

GEORGE ROGER RICHARD LE PORTE

Re-rolled Havana
$8.00 $9.00

All soft work advance of $1.00
Extreme shapes no less than $10.00

But, if the said Board of Arbitration, from such examination, shall determine that the cities and places which compete with the city of Binghamton in the markets of the country are not paying higher wages than are demanded by the cigarmakers of the city of Binghamton, agree to work at the same prices for which they were working when they went out on strike."

Dated: Binghamton, New York, August 1st, 1890

/s/ James Wood
John Doyle
Edward Dundon
Frank Hunt
Mary F. J. Kelly

Mr. Wales then made it clear that they, the manufacturers, would "not meet in any matters" with the representatives of the Cigarmakers International Union. Since Messers. Dundon and Doyle were union organizers; he requested that they be excluded from all future meetings. He went on to say, "the sole object of the union in advocating and agitating this strike was not because they cared anything for the question of wages, but with the sole idea of making Binghamton 'a union town'."

Senator O'Connor, attorney for the manufacturers, reiterated his colleague's remarks and stated that the manufacturers would absolutely decline to meet with the union, or any committee composed in whole or in part of its representatives, "even if their factories were forced to remain closed for five years."

Rumors began to circulate through the rank and file of the striking workers that their union representatives from the International had been bought out by the manufacturers. Accusations went back and forth. The union leadership went on to explain to the working men and women that this was a well known tactic created by the employers to discredit the union and bring about dissention in the ranks. They went on to say that the workers must stay firm in their demands. They should not listen to the rumors, but rather, try to find out where these rumors had come from.

These accusations were brought to the Arbitration table, as were accusations that the arbitrator Mr. Donovan was a dupe of the manufacturers.

At the next meeting it was made known that Messers. Dundon and Doyle would no longer serve on the committee, and too, with respect to the question that was raised as to Mr. Donovan's impartiality. Mr. Donovan flatly contradicted the rumor that he had been invited or instigated to attend this conference by the manufacturers. He stated further that he was there voluntarily and pursuant to his official duties. The meeting was adjourned when Mr. Donovan made it known that his findings would be made known, in accordance with the law, after thirty days of investigation by him.

As the strike wore on into August, with no prospect for a settlement in view, the number of arrests on conspiracy charges increased. Typical examples were arrests and fines of twenty-five dollars for violation of a city ordnance against assembling without a permit. On August 21st, five pickets were sentenced to serve one hundred days in the Albany penitentiary on the complaint of Charles A. Hull, and, on the same day union organizer George Mc Guire was arrested on a warrant issued by the Supreme Court charging him with conspiracy.

On August 23rd, Senator O'Connor, attorney for the manufacturers, obtained a restraining order issued by Judge Gerritt A. Forbes, of the Supreme Court in Syracuse "restraining striking cigarmakers and others from interfering with the interests of the cigar manufacturers."

Following this, the striking cigarmakers received a mortal blow when an injunction was served on the strikers. The State Board of Arbitration had done nothing! This was swiftly followed by a Writ of Restraint issued by Judge Charles E. Parker of the Supreme Court, which charged the strikers for being engaged in an illegal conspiracy.

The manufacturers, after ten weeks, made their position clear through the statement of Mr. Charles Hull when he said, "We will eat just as many meals and lose no sleep over it. We can stand it longer than the ignorant masses."

A further injustice was the accusation made by a striker, Harris Frank, that Mr. Charles Hull had approached him and caned him while he was on picket duty. Nothing was done to Mr. Hull. The police merely replied that the case would be investigated.

A meeting of the strikers was called for at Cigarmakers Hall on the sixth of October. The following statement was read to the people in attendance:

To the striking cigarmakers of the City of Binghamton—we as members of the strike committee, elected by a majority vote of the cigarmakers who went on strike fifteen weeks ago deem it our duty, at the present crisis in our affairs, to lay before the body a statement of our condition, and to leave it to the good judgment of a majority to decide whether you consider it advisable to continue your struggle for a just increase in wages, or whether you will declare the strike off for the present.

The strike has been of such unexpected duration; the preparation was so inadequate that many of our people have become extremely destitute, and while the amount of money, which has been received, has been creditable to the sympathies of organized labor throughout the country, it is far from sufficient to support the needy.

There is now, on our relief list, one thousand one hundred persons, eight hundred receiving aid continually, the remainder of them occasionally. Since the strike began we have received in voluntary contributions twenty thousand dollars, an average of one thousand three hundred thirty-three dollars per week, or a dollar twenty-two cents for each person receiving aid.

There are now, in the factories four hundred eleven persons, of these two hundred seventy-five are Apprentices and one hundred thirty-six are old workmen, some of whom were strikers and have been forced by circumstances unwillingly to return to work. The rest are Pennsylvania "independent workmen."

The manufacturers are having their more urgent orders filled in Schenevus, Buffalo and New York."

A vote was called for and the outcome was one hundred sixty-seven for calling the strike off and one hundred fifty-five to continue.

It was reported in the Binghamton Weekly Leader that people cried bitterly. Calls for a recount could be heard throughout the hall. Pandemonium broke loose. The count remained. The strike was over and the workers returned to their places of employment.

* * * * * *

While all of the events of the strike were going on, Bella had settled into her office position under the sharp-eyes and quick hands of Miss. Ives. Bella was a quick learner and Miss. Ives had immediately taken a liking to her. In fact, after a month on the job, Miss. Ives told Bella that she could call her by her Christian name, Hazel instead of the formal Miss. Ives.

Although Bella started out with simple task of filing papers, it didn't take Miss Ives long to see that Bella was a very bright young lady who caught on to things very quickly. She progressed to some simple bookkeeping tasks with the posting of the accounts receivable and payable. Miss Ives had instructed Bella that you never paid for anything immediately.

BELLA

You should wait the full thirty or sixty days so that your money in the bank made money for you as long as it could. This was something new for Bella to understand. But it didn't taker her long to realize that banks were there for the folks who wanted to save money.

Miss Ives sat Bella down one afternoon and told her that she really should acquire more skills in order to be the complete person that she could become. After all, Miss Ives said, "I'll be retiring soon and you will be perfect to take over for me." But first, you must go to night school and learn how to type and to learn how to take shorthand. School is free and I will help you if you should have any problems,"

Bella spoke to Mama about this and many of the other things she was learning under the tutelage of Miss. Ives. She also asked Mama to allow her to go to Night School to learn how to use a typewriter. She convinced mama that she could advance on the job faster and better if she could acquire that skill. Mama agreed. She added that learning was very important.

When Bella went to sign up for Night School she learned that she could take a course in Bookkeeping and Shorthand at the same time.

Bella couldn't get over the number of adults who were taking classes. There were those who were studying to become citizens. There were those who were learning to read and write. But, most of all there were folks who had become impacted from the strike of cigarmakers and wanted to obtain some skills that could lead them out of the rut of being a factory worker.

One evening during a break between classes she bumped into a middle-aged gentleman while standing in the corridor. They got to talking inasmuch as Bella thought it strange that someone in their forties would think about going to school. She learned from Mr. Stewart that he was a toolmaker, but he had always wanted to become a teacher. He had learned that there might be an opportunity for him in the newly created vocational school that the city was opening. Since they had no criteria for obtaining skilled teachers in the various vocational fields, the city was looking for talented and skilled workmen to apply for a job in which they would teach their skills to help train young boys and girls to fill the needs of the various businesses that were moving into the Greater Binghamton area.

They got to know each other quite well over the weeks. Mr. Stewart informed Bella that he had five children, three boys and two girls. He was determined that they would go to school and finish their education as far as they could go. He didn't want to see them end up like him having to struggle to get ahead later in life. Bill Stewart was a great influence on Bella. He echoed the words spoken by Mama that virtually said how education is the stepping-stone out of poverty for the people of the middle class. He also pointed out the tremendous opportunities that one has in America. "It doesn't matter," he said, "who you are or where you came from. If you have the skills that are needed you can elevate yourself to a better level of social class. People who don't take advantage of the system are foolish. After all, he would say, where else can you get an education for free?"

Bella heeded this advice and studied very hard. In spite of the fact that the Gregg-Pittman class seemed very confusing with all of the symbols that actually were words she was able to graduate at the head of her class in all of the disciplines that she had studied. The skills that she had acquired served her well with Miss. Ives. Mamma was proud along with Miss Westcott who doted over her accomplishments!

One day, Mr. Westcott came into the office and asked for Miss. Ives. Bella told him that she had just stepped out but perhaps she could help him. He responded by saying he didn't think so, however, he replied that he needed to see an invoice from one of his New York suppliers. Bella went quickly to the file cabinet and retrieved the invoice. Mr. Westcott was surprised. I suppose you can also type me a letter. She acknowledged that she could and sat down in front of the typewriter ready to accommodate Mr. Westcott's needs. When he had finished dictating the letter he took a good look at Bella. He said, "Don't I know you? You look very familiar to me, but I don't recall noticing you here around the office."

Bella responded by telling him that she was the person his daughter asked him to place on the job in his office and pointed out that she was also the girl who played the piano at several of his wife's recitals. She added that she was very grateful to him and his family for providing her with so many opportunities. Just then Miss. Ives returned from the ladies room and was pleased that Bella had been able to fill Mr. Westcott's needs in her absence. She wasn't the least bit jealous. In fact, she was very proud of the way her young protégé responded. She knew, then, that she had taught her well. There was no doubt in anyone's mind that Bella would fit in.

* * * * * *

After the strike, the depression of 1893 affected all areas of manufacture.

The failure of the English financial house of Baring Brothers in 1890 as a result of gold mining enterprises in South Africa and speculation in Argentine securities, seriously affected the United States. This had impacted on the manufacturers of Binghamton since one of the Baring brothers had married the daughter of William Bingham the founder of Binghamton. Understandably, Mr., Baring had a profound affect upon the investors of Binghamton so that when the Baring enterprise went under so did many of the investors of Binghamton. The financial problems that followed forced English investors to sell their American securities. The events were so disturbing that Mr. Baring returned to England. He could no longer face his friends to whom he had given advice. He later died in Bath, England.

The failure of the Philadelphia and Reading Railroad in February and the National Cordage Company in May ushered in the Panic of 1893.

The Erie, Northern Pacific and other railroads followed the Philadelphia and Reading into bankruptcy until one-fourth of the railroad capital was in receivership.

The prolonged and paralyzing strike of cigarmakers in Binghamton pointed out the deep-rooted struggle between labor and management so typical of this period. It can be readily understood why the further appeal of new industries and higher wages forced the cigar industry into its final phase of decline.

* * * * * *

Around 1895 the old-time prosperity returned to Binghamton and cigar manufacturing. In that year sixty-five firms and proprietors were engaged in the manufacture of cigars. By 1899 the number of manufacturers rose to seventy. It was estimated that at least five thousand employees were at work with an average weekly payroll of forty to fifty thousand dollars varying from five dollars a week paid to unskilled labor to about fifteen dollars paid to skilled men. The annual number of cigars was estimated at three million.

* * * * * *

Miss Westcott, the schoolteacher, still invited Bella to their home along with David who was growing up to be quite a bright young man.

During this time, Bella had listened very carefully to the conversations and discussions that the business partners and friends of Mr. Westcott were having both in and out of the office. There was always a great deal of conversation regarding the stock market as well as the gossip surrounding the embarrassment of their friend Mr. Baring. Despite the Depression there was much wealth to be made if one invested wisely.

Bella invested her savings wisely and was beginning to show a wealth beyond her wildest belief. The family had never changed their way of living so that no one had even suspected that the family was becoming one of the wealthiest immigrant families in their neighborhood. Neither Uncle Louis nor Aunt Sadie ever suspected what was happening either. Mama, grandfather, and the kids went about their business as if nothing had changed.

Aunt Sadie had some suspicions, however, when it was decided that Bella's brother Abraham would go on to high school and later to college.

Bella's brother, Abraham, had wanted to become a lawyer. Aunt Sadie had wondered how all of this was going to be financed. But, because Abraham was quite smart she accepted the idea that he would be able to attend college on a scholarship. What made that notion seem credible was the fact that Abraham was easily accepted as a Freshman at Cornell University.

Abraham's dorm was Risley where he waited on tables to help pay for his food. He described the dining hall to Bella and Mama in a letter shortly after he arrived on campus.

If he had wanted to eat he had to be in the dining hall by 6:00 a.m. Serving of the students began at 6:30! That didn't give the servers much time to eat their breakfast.

Each server had two tables to serve. There were nine students to a table. The china that they served the food on was very heavy. Lugging a tray was a chore. There were always a minimum of eighteen plates every time you carried a tray. You also didn't want to break any of the china nor did you want any to turn up missing.

All of the china was counted at the beginning and end of

the year. If there were any pieces missing all of the servers had to pay a portion of their wages toward the reimbursement of the missing pieces. Because of this, you also had to be careful not to drop any of the trays while you were serving.

The servers had to watch the students very carefully because of the beautiful engraving of the Tower Crest on the dishes. The chinaware made for great souvenirs!

The dining room, as Abraham described it, was spectacular. It had a high ceiling. They were told that it was a replica of Christ Church in Oxford, England. Abraham went on to say that on Sunday the students were allowed to smoke. It took all week for the smoke to clear since it had climbed to the top of the dome and lingered there.

There was a great camaraderie among the servers. Some of the servers that had been there before showed the newcomers, when they had the first snow, that they could use the trays to slide down the hill outside of Risley. That was fun!

Serving the evening meal was difficult because you had to be in the dining room by four-thirty and that was just about the time, on certain days, that Abraham got out of his last class on the other side of the campus. He didn't get to eat legally on those days. The servers that had been there before showed them how to order seconds for their table and be able to eat a meal for themselves.

Classes were difficult. It was especially difficult in the math, chemistry, and physics classes since the professors were very demanding. Abraham knew that he had to work extra hard because he did not want to let the family down. He knew how hard they had sacrificed for him, especially his sister Bella. He assured Mama and Bella that he was indeed working as hard as he could. He was not about to let anyone down. He would succeed! And he did! He was accepted at the Cornell School of Law after completing his undergraduate studies where he excelled.

* * * * * *

After the strike had ended, important innovations were introduced into the manufacture of cigars. Employers bent on not having a repetition of the strike began to introduce machinery into their plants.

On August 18, 1897, a charter was granted to the Cigarmakers' Union #16 and the Cigarmakers' Union #218 by President Samuel Gompers and Frank Morrison, Secretary of the American Federation of Labor. The charter for the Central Labor Union called for the organization of all labor.

The following month, "The Blue Label," the union label of which the Binghamton cigarmakers were a participating member appeared in Binghamton.

Edward J. Smith, the organizer of the Cigarmakers International Union spoke before an assemblage of workers in Binghamton. He told them, "The cigarmakers Union has been in existence since 1864. It was reorganized on an advanced practical union plan in 1879. We have today, twenty-nine thousand members who pay thirty cents per week, for which they receive the following benefits: When out of work, three dollars per week; when sick, five dollars per week; death of a wife, forty dollars for burial expenses; death of a member, life insurance running from fifty dollars to five hundred fifty dollars according to the length of membership of the deceased.

We also have a loan system. Members may borrow, without interest, to the sum of twenty dollars, while seeking work, traveling from city to city. This they pay back at the rate of ten per cent of their weekly earnings when employed.

Smith added that the out-of-work benefits paid in 1895 amounted to one hundred sixty-six thousand, three hundred seventy-seven dollars and twenty-five cents. Sick benefits paid amounted to one hundred twelve thousand five hundred sixty-seven dollars and six cients. Death claims amounted to sixty-six thousand seven hundred twenty-five dollars and ninety-eight cents. Loans amounted to forty-one thousand six hundred seventy-five dollars and sixteen cents. While strike benefits amounted to forty-four thousand thirty-nine dollars and six cents for a grand total of four hundred thirty-one thousand three hundred sixty-six dollars and fifty-one cents in total benefits!

Smith went on to say, "Now, the last two years of the financial depression has been great, causing large factories to shut down so that we paid out a little over nine hundred thousand dollars during that period."

"In the past sixteen years we have paid a grand total of over three million dollars and we hold today a little over a quarter of a million dollars in our reserve fund."

"The Cigarmakers International have a copyrighted label, being blue in color and protected by laws of nearly every state in the United States and Canada. This blue label guarantees, to the public, the cigar bearing this trademark on the box will smoke free. That they are not made in any filthy tenement houses, or by convicts, or by Chinese, but are made by the best workmen, under fair conditions, and in clean factories and that the cigars are of the best grade."

By 1905, an innovation was introduced. The Binghamton John B. Rogers and Company was the originator and most successful exponent of the "factory to smoker" plan of cigar-manufacturing and selling.

Through magazine advertising, Rogers had established an extensive mail-order business shipping his cigars to the consumer on a "money-back if not satisfactory" plan. His motto was, "Printers Ink My Only Salesman." Another motto was, "We will save you half your cigar money!"

The company claimed over fifty-thousand regular customers and employed one hundred twenty-five workers with an output of about five million cigars a year.

Although competition was fierce there were many factories that flourished.

The Frank A. Bronson Company employed five salesmen and produced three million cigars a year. Ferdinand B. Richards employed two hundred hands and was the largest factory in Binghamton employing exclusively skilled union help and was the third largest factory in the United States. All of their cigars bore the union blue label.

The Barnes Smith and Company employed five salesmen and employed six hundred hands.

Two of the most prominent cigar-box companies, an

outgrowth of the cigar industry, were the Binghamton Cigar Box Company that manufactured twenty-five thousand boxes each week and employed between forty and sixty workers. The Lacy Cigar Box factory boasted on having modern machinery. The machines consisted of five power nailing machines and four printing presses! Their printing presses were able to print four thousand to eight thousand impressions an hour and through the use of steam they were able to produce three thousand to seven thousand boxes per day.

The Charles Westcott Company and the Woodruff Cigar Box Company were not far behind. They too became mechanized through the latest machinery.

When Miss Ives retired, Bella became the person in charge of the office and the closest confidante to Mr. Westcott. He trusted her implicitly. Bella had proven to be a truly intelligent and industrious woman. In fact, there were times when Mr. Westcott would call Bella into his inner office and ask her for advice on many of the things that were going through his mind including the possibility of moving toward machine technology.

Bella was quick to respond. Despite the fact that machines would replace many of her friends, and particularly Aunt Sadie, she knew that the way to progress and greater income for the company was in that direction. They talked for many hours as Mr. Westcott agonized over the prospect of having to replace many of his loyal workers, particularly the older ones, with machines.

Bella offered him a solution. "Keep your older workers,"

she said, "inasmuch as they have a wealth of knowledge and experience. Use them as mentors to the new wave of younger employees who will be learning the intricacies of the machines. Together you will have a marriage of the best of both worlds. Then as the older workers retire you will be left with a work force full of the knowledge of the old and the new."

Her advice seemed so sound that Charles Westcott began to embark in that direction. His factory became one of the leading manufacturers of the day by producing more than six million cigars a year.

In the process, his dear friend and business associate, Mr. Woodruff, the producer of his cigar boxes became mechanized too, producing seven thousand boxes each day.

Although Woodruff and Westcott held almost daily conferences Bella's path had never crossed that of Richard who had already begun work, starting at his father's factory, and then embarking with his own office as a prominent attorney in the Binghamton area. In fact, he had been mentioned as a new up-and-comer in the ranks of the Republican Party.

Over the years, Richard Woodruff had become well-liked by all with whom he had come into contact. He was dashingly handsome and considered quite a catch by the parents of every girl known within the family circle. The girls fawned over him. His mother and father were quick to remind him that it was high time for him to find a suitable fiancé to settle down with. In fact, Mrs. Woodruff had already had some intimate discussions with Mrs. Brady of the Brady Banking family. As a result, Richard was paired with Emily Brady at all of the functions that the families were a part of. Mr. And Mrs. Woodruff both agreed that Emily Brady would be the perfect partner for Richard. Richard was also reminded that Mr. Brady was Chairman of the Broome County Republican Party and had many friends in high places. Even though the Republican Party had had a split at the Chicago Convention when it had ruled out Theodore Roosevelt delegates in favor of President Taft, that split had little or no impact on New York State and more specifically Broome County.

The following Christmas, the formal engagement of Richard Woodruff to Miss. Emily Brady was announced, at the Country Club, much to no one's surprise but to the disappointment of many of the eligible ladies from their social group. The wedding was scheduled for the Spring.

Bella caught sight of the announcement in the Society Section of the Broome County Republican. Bella knew that this announcement would be coming. She heard a lot of the conversation and rumors at the office. And, there wasn't a week gone by when Richard and Emily's faces did not appear in the Sunday Rotogravure section of the newspaper. They were quite the couple with Richard being quite the catch!

Richard's name began to be linked in the political arena. With the help of his father-in-law Richard was able to get on the Republican ticket as a County Legislator. He won the election handily. It wasn't long after that his name came up to be a candidate for a State office. There was an opening coming in the State Legislature. Mr. Brady knew that there would be a distinct power base for him and his cronies if Richard could get himself entrenched in State politics. With the help of the

Party Richard was elected to the Assembly. He served on the banking committee and was able to help his father-in-law and his father-in-laws friends with insights and information that was not readily available to the average investors. Harvey Westcott was among his father-in-laws confidantes. As such he was able to foresee the direction that business and industry was going. The information he received helped him to make the right decisions so that his firm would become one of the survivors.

Bella was privy to all of the discussions that were held in the Westcott office. She was able to make some very wise investments for herself and her family. She was beginning to grow very wealthy indeed. Still, no one was the wiser. She did not flaunt her wealth. Bella continued to live with her mother and grandfather. There was always enough for all. Even when Uncle Louis and Aunt Sadie had faced some financial difficulties when they tried to put their children through college, Bella was there to help. After all, she told Mama. Family is family! Bella also remembered how Uncle Louis and Aunt Sadie took their family into their home when they arrived in America. With no strings attached financial help was there.

In the meantime, David was becoming a young man in his own right. David was the number one student in all of his classes. Miss. Westcott took quite a shine to him and was heard to remark that David was as bright as his mother! His thirst for knowledge was seen in the fact that he was always full of questions. His quest for answers showed his perseverant qualities that made Miss. Westcott feel certain that he would one day go to college and that he would excel in whatever he chose to do.

David was number one is his classes at elementary school. But, in addition to the academics it was also clear that David excelled in sports, too. It was mandatory to take classes in Physical education. David especially liked Basketball and Baseball. His gym teacher, Mr. Thomas, spent a great deal of time with David since David was bright as well as proficient. When David graduated from elementary school his gym teacher, Mr. Thomas had already spoken to the high school coaches. David's skills allowed him to make it to the Varsity teams as a freshman, something that didn't happen too often. By the time David was a Junior he was elected Captain by the other players and led them to the city championships in both basketball and baseball.

At an early age David voiced an interest in the law. He announced when he was five that he was destined to become a great lawyer and politician. Someday, he told Bella, he would make her proud. Certainly his grades in high school underscored his dreams. He graduated as Valedictorian of his class. More importantly, he was liked not only by his teachers but especially by his classmates. David was like by all!

* * * * * *

By 1907, Binghamton was third in annual output of cigars among the cigar manufacturing cities in the United States with an annual output of over one hundred twenty-five million cigars.

By 1909, their annual output was up to one hundred fifty

million cigars. But, the manufacturers were quoted as saying, "We would largely increase this output if we could get the right kind of help."

The manufacturers were referring to the fact that the great influx of union men with union wages were hampering the growth of the cigar industry in Binghamton.

In the Lancaster sections of Pennsylvania workmen who were in direct competition with the Binghamton workers were still bringing their tobacco home with them and working after quitting time in their kitchens sometimes putting their entire families to work.

This was a practice that was outlawed in New York State by the Health and Bonding Laws. However, the scale of wages and hours was not yet fixed by law in Pennsylvania enabling the manufacturer to compete very favorably with the Binghamton factories.

According to the 1900 census, the number of women and children employed in Binghamton cigar factories was 5.4% of the total population, against 3.9% in Elmira, and 1.58% in the United States as a whole.

Putting the matter another way, 40% of the five thousand six hundred thirty-six Binghamton wage earners were reported by that census to be women, and about two-thirds of them to be working in the cigar factories.

* * * * * *

There were other events forming a cloud over the heads of the immigrants of that community. There was a crisis taking place in Europe where most of them had come from.

BELLA

Folks read with consternation of the assassination of Archduke Francis Ferdinand, heir to the Austrian throne, by the Bosnian revolutionary student, Gavrilo Princip.

William the Second had been preaching the glorification of force and the idea of a German Kultur and Deutschland über Alles (Germany forever). As a result the world was holding its breath not knowing when Germany might jump into a fight. It was thought that the Kaiser truly believed that Russia, France and England were trying to encircle him.

Austria gave Serbia an ultimatum on the pretext that Serbia was responsible for the crime. And, despite the fact that Serbia's ally was Russia, Austria had no fear of reprisal inasmuch as Germany was her ally.

The old Europeans were well aware that if Germany did come to the aid of Austria then England and France would have to support their ally Russia. All of this saber-rattling had the earmarks of war. Of this they were certain, there was going to be a war!

It didn't take long. Uncle Louis was reading the newspaper, one morning, before heading out to work. He read to Aunt Sadie that the newspapers were reporting that the Germans had invaded Belgium. Several days later Liege fell. It seemed that the Germans had brought up a super weapon called the "Big Bertha." It was a gun that crushed the fortresses from a very large distance away minimizing the casualties on the German side. Aunt Sadie remarked to Uncle Louis, "Why doesn't somebody stop them?" Days later it was reported that bombs were being dropped on Paris. Newspapers were reporting that the armies of the Allies were in retreat. In Russia it was being reported that von Hindenburg was pushing the Russians back.

Officially President Woodrow Wilson had declared that the United States would maintain a position of neutrality. American neutrality after the first few weeks of war was largely technical. There were few Americans who did not take sides.

Germany in the beginning had many sympathizers. Families, in this country, had become split over this issue. Mama's neighbor Tante Salg had heated arguments with her sister Tante Berg over the rights of the German people to have their place in the sun, just as the British had boasted was theirs. Also, Tante Berg would contend that, America was not being neutral when they sold munitions and supplies to the Allies and not to the Germans.

The rise of German militarism and their propaganda regarding world conquest attracted the fancy of the German people both here in America as well as in Germany. Inasmuch as the government was dominated by the military class and was supported by the financial, commercial and industrialists who saw an opportunity for great profits it was easy to convince the people that they were following the right course of action.

Although these differences prevailed among the American people, once again, the notion that they were over there and we're over here gave comfort to the American people. On the whole, however, American sympathies lay more with the Allies than with Germany.

The invasion of Belgium had a great impact on American

feelings. The atrocities that were reported almost daily in the newspapers along with the bombing of churches, building that were landmarks known to all, as well as innocent people, were evidence of a cruelty not to be forgiven by Americans who had harbored feelings of fair play and peace.

This was the formal position of the United States until German submarines had interfered with American shipping on the high seas. The final nail in Germany's coffin came over the sinking of the passenger ship Lusitania off the coast of Ireland by a German submarine. According to newspaper reports no warning was given to the many Americans who were on board. The United States became involved too.

President Woodrow Wilson declared war! Americans had entered World War I with enthusiasm. The Americans had entered the war as if it were a high and holy Crusade. The slogan of the time was that America was fighting to make the world safe for democracy rather than the autocracy being offered by the German vermacht,

Aunt Sadie found herself taking up Red Cross work along with Bella. Every Tuesday night they would roll bandages in their synagogue's basement as their contribution for the war effort.

In the period of 1914 to 1918 the cigar manufacturing plants could not keep up with the demands brought about through World War I.

The average worker worked eleven hours a day, five and a half days a week, for a twenty dollar gold piece.

It was during this period that the "big three" made their

appearance in Binghamton, –American Cigar, General Cigar and Consolidated Cigar. Their appearance introduced the corporation amid the heretofore family-type structure.

During this period too, the phenomenal growth of the shoe industry in this area provided a larger and more stabilizing factor in employment. Boots and shoes were needed by the military. There was plenty of work for everyone. Indeed, Lestershire, now Johnson City, and Endicott owed their development entirely to the shoe industry.

Germany had underestimated the resisting power of the French Republic. They also had no concept of the role that Great Britain and the United States were to play. By the end of the war Americans had adopted a spirit of isolationism. Many Americans became disillusioned by the fact that the victors could not agree on many of the fundamental issues they faced. The American people began to see themselves as not wanting to have anything to do with Europe although many of their forbears had come from Europe. Unfortunately, it wasn't long before the United States was drawn into the war. Abraham, who had a dear friend, Harold Steinberg, in the ROTC at Cornell, decided that he would go with his friend and enlist in the army. Harold had told Abraham that Cornell grads were receiving a Lieutenant's commission and he would join with the American Expeditionary Force.

Abraham announced to mama that he was proud to be an American and it was his duty to respond to the call! After all, this country had given them a good home with the kind of security that they had never had before. This country also gave him the opportunity to be able to go to school and get the best education possible. There was much to be thankful for, Abraham repeated! Abraham promised mama that he would write to her and let her know what was happening to him. Mama cried for many days but Abraham had made up his mind.

David was so proud of his "brother." David had always looked up to Abraham and he especially listened when Abraham told him how important school was. David promised Abraham that he would make him proud. He still had visions of becoming a lawyer.

Alex's first letter to mama told her that he and the other recruits had taken their basic training at Camp McCain in Mississippi. It was quite a shock. It was almost like being in another world. Although this was still America, the culture of the people was so radically different. The recruits, Alex said, learned to march, shoot and work together as a group whenever the order was given. After Camp McCain the group returned to Camp Shanks in New York. Camp Shanks was a few miles up the Hudson from New York City. This camp was a port of embarkation (POE) for troops leaving for Europe. We went through a maze of processing, Alex wrote, getting shots in the arm, having clothes checked, as well as instructions on boat drills in case something should happen on the way over. After all, it was widely known that German submarines patrolled the Atlantic hoping to discover troop transports and those ships carrying supplies to the Allies.

We were at Camp Shanks for five days. We boarded trains that went to the docks of New York City. We had to carry, what seemed to us, tons of equipment. We were wearing woolen uniforms (OD's) as such we felt as though we would suffocate from the heat. All of the men were given a number that designated where they would be while on board the ship. Lt. Carter, the First Sergeant and I had numbers 1, 2, and 3 however we were the last ones to get to our rooms because we had to call the roll and check the men of the battery as they stepped from the gangplank to the boat-room. The real good thing that happened here was that the Red Cross was on hand to give us lemonade and donuts. A much needed aperitif!

In the morning, we sailed out of New York Harbor and got our first and last look at that dear old lady, the Statue of Liberty. I cannot begin to describe the feelings that arose in me as I looked at the skyline of New York and at the Statue of Liberty. During the next half hour I think that I went over my entire past life. But, as the city faded into the distance and the endless expanse of water closed in around us we started to look around the ship we were on in order to get our bearings. We knew we would be stuck here for several days!

There were hundreds of men on board and each was assigned to a certain section of the ship. They were not permitted to leave that section to go to another section. Ours was one deck higher than the water and at all times during the day we could look out of the port hole. Many of the men slept on the decks or in bunks and took turns sleeping. This had to be done so that all could be as comfortable as possible under such crowded conditions. Meals were served by the numbers. When your number was called you were fed. If you missed your number you had to go without until the next meal which would be about five hours away! I had no trouble with this rule as I had a friend who was assigned to KP duty and I would slip in through the kitchen door and eat heartily whenever I felt like it. However, the food was of a poor quality but substantial enough to keep us going through the entire trip. Many of the men stuck slices of bread in their pockets so that they could eat it later during the trip.

The early part of the evenings were spent on deck by most of the men. At 9 o'clock, each night, all of the ports and decks were closed because of blackout regulations. The rest of the evenings we spent in our assigned areas playing cards, singing, reading or telling jokes.

The sea was quite calm during the entire voyage and very few men got sick. The boat was large so that there was scarcely no roll and that also helped. We were unescorted all the way, but all of the guns were manned and a sharp lookout for enemy subs or ships was kept.

As we approached Europe it got colder and colder and we were very glad, now, to have the woolen uniforms and jackets to wear. The time was changed each night, moving the clock ahead one hour each time, until we had advanced six hours by the time we had reached our destination. One morning we got our first glimpse of land. At first just a little rise in the water and gradually growing until the outline became more distinct, and we could distinguish the patches of color and objects that later proved to be houses. We didn't know what land this was but the word soon got around that this was Ireland. By now, we had begun to see many ships of all sizes and large convoys carrying all the materials of war. All that day we had very interesting scenery to look at and it was quite a relief after looking at nothing but water for the last several days. However, I must say, there is something awe-inspiring in looking over the rail of a ship and watching the water as it is pushed aside by the prow of the ship.

The weather was wonderful all the time except for one day when we ran into a thunderstorm. But, that too was a new experience for the majority of us and we enjoyed it. As the day wore on and evening came, we approached the shore which was now on both sides of us because we were sailing up the Firth of Clyde in Scotland. The sunset was magnificent and the scenery too beautiful to describe. To me, it was worth all the trying time I had been through just to be there just to see this wonderful sight. The houses of the towns along the waterfront were odd and really like the pictures on the postcards that one seldom sees with his own eyes.

The big ship had finally come to a stop even though we all had the feeling that it was still moving. Now came the task of unloading the cargo along with the men who had gotten sick along the way. Small boats came alongside and we watched from the rail barrier until it got dark and we had to go below. We spent that night on board the ship even though it was in the harbor and at anchor. The next morning we prepared to leave, We left in the order that we had come on board. As we drew onto the dock we could hear the strains of bagpipes coming from a Scottish band. They drew closer and we could see their costumes and their bagpipes hung over their shoulders. They were very happy to see us and cheered as we crossed over to where our train was waiting to take us to our final destination, England.

BELLA

I have often read about and seen in movies the type of trains and cars that are used in the countries of Europe but never expected to be riding in one and never under the conditions we were now in. I was assigned to a compartment with five other men. Red Cross workers passed through and gave us coffee and donuts for which we were most thankful since we were very hungry at this point. The train finally started and we settled down for our journey across the British Isles. No one knew where we were going. The night was spent on the train which made stops along the way. When we were allowed to get out and stretch, we were given some more coffee and doughnuts, that the people very generously gave to us at the stations.

At about five in the morning we arrived at a blackout station in England that proved to be the end of our train ride. We unloaded here and mounted up into trucks that whisked us off into the darkness. We didn't have far to go, however, and were unloaded. We were formed into ranks and the Captain talked to us and told us of the situation for the time being.

The entire battery was staged at this place and remained there for three weeks. Three weeks of preparing and getting our equipment read for that day when we would once more set sail for a foreign shore. This time it would be Europe itself which in the days to come would hold so much for all of us and which was to be the final resting place of so many of our comrades. But, we all looked forward to a job that had to be done, no matter what the cost, and with the bringing of freedom to all the people overrun by the Hun Terrorists.

Early in the morning, one month to the date we left the

states, we pulled out and travelled across the southern part of England to the coastal town of Weymouth where we spent the night. The next morning we boarded the boats that were to take us across the channel to France. Trucks were chained to the decks and secured against any possible rough weather or possibly enemy action. This time there were quite a few ships with a strong escort. The channel was very calm and we were a little disappointed because we had heard so much about how rough it would be. As we approached the coastline of France we could hear the sound of guns firing and it was exciting. All we could see was a desolate strip of sandy beach as we were drawing in to the shore, but beyond that was destruction. Destruction of all the trees, hedgerows and nearly everything else, including many pieces of equipment enemy and allied. Now came the task of unloading again only this time there was no dock or boat to meet us. We disembarked onto the beach and in many cases into the war! One again everything went smoothly and orderly and we found ourselves up a muddy road in France.

As the convoy of trucks was formed we moved ahead until finally we were traveling along the road at a good rate of speed. Now we could really see the destruction along the way and we realized the terrific fight that those who preceded us had had to wage when they made their landing. Next came an assembly point in a field where we stopped the trucks and had a bite to eat. It was in this field that we saw our first German mine and looked at some of the fortifications that had been built by them to guard the coast against an invasion. We were warned not to touch anything and to be very careful where we walked. But, there was no need for the warning as we were all so-called "rookies" and expected anything.

After lunch we moved out onto the road again and traveled inland. The further inland we went the more destruction we could see as we had to pass through towns that were completely destroyed. The names were strange to us. Avaranches, Carentan, Caen, Fougeres and many others not found on maps but contained many houses, of French people, that were now completely devastated. The people cheered and waved throwing apples and flowers at us as we passed by. We couldn't help but feel we were truly "saviours" as they called us.

We spent that night and the next in an apple orchard just outside the city of Rennes. Now began the work of setting up my field desk, making entries into my log that the men had arrived in Europe, and all the other necessary functions that need to wind up in the Adjutant General's Department in Washington. So far everything was going along very smoothly. But, of course, we were all very tense. We immediately dug our foxholes and prepared for whatever was in store.

Several days later we were on the move. I shall never forget the briefing we received by our commanding officer prior to our departure. "This is it, he said, "the Krauts have the area zeroed in and the minute we pull into the area dig in and dig in fast. Load your carbines and shoot the first son-of-a-bitch that is not a friendly." We slept in the trenches that we had dug. Every night a plane would fly overhead. We named it Bed-check Charlie. It was a Jerry plane that would fly over our area in order to get info as to exactly where our troops were in order that the German guns could be more accurate. Fortunately for us most of the shells went flying over our heads and landed on the other side of us killing some of the French people and their animals.

The Christmas season came and we all celebrated as best we could. Some of the men cut down a little fir tree and made decorations to put on it and so the Christmas spirit was there. The Jewish soldiers called it "our Chanukah bush."

New Year's Day came. Some of the French who lived nearby gave us their wine and we drank to the old year and wished for victory during the new. For some, the next day proved to be a rather sick one. But, as the old saying goes, "It was worth it."

We were very lucky. So far, we had only lost one man!

I have to stop for now. We have just received our alert orders to go into battle. Tell Grandfather, Bella and David that I love them dearly and think of them all of the time. Tell David, especially, to get good grades in school and prepare for college. When I get home we can open up our own law firm.

That was the only letter mama had received from Alex. Shortly after it had come, mama received a telegram from the war department that Abraham, a gallant soldier, was killed in action. It added that he had been awarded the Bronze Star, Silver Star and Purple Heart for his gallantry.

Mama was never the same. She was devastated over her loss.

Everything went smoothly and efficiently. By the end of World War I, and through the period of the twenties, two important developments occurred. Small factories were being bought out by the rapidly expanding corporations, and heavy machinery was being introduced into the industry. The owners of factories found it necessary to put tremendous amounts of capital into their businesses if they expected to continue.

One by one the cigar manufacturers in Binghamton sold out to "the big three."

By the end of the twenties the only "old timers " left were Hull-Grummond Company and Harvey Westcott.

Harvey Westcott was a shrewd businessman who saw the need to diversify. He was quick to pick up with the newest company to arrive into the Binghamton area. Harvey had developed a friendship with young Otto Farben, son of the large German conglomerate I.G. Farben. Young Otto, through the advice and help of Harvey Westcott bought out the old General Cigar factory.

American Tobacco and Consolidated Cigar had already left Binghamton due to the increasing number of labor laws that were passed in New York State. The cost of doing business on the small margin of profit was too costly even for the large corporations, and by 1934 the General Cigar Company left and set up new factories in Pennsylvania where strict labor laws were not in effect.

Harvey saw this as an outstanding opportunity to get rid of the competition and at the same time invest in this new I. G. Farben Company that was called Ansco.

Harvey was quick to invest in this fledgling company and so did Bella.

It was especially evident to Harvey that here was a "gold mine" in its infancy. Ansco had just won a landmark patent struggle in the roll film process against Eastman Kodak from Rochester, New York that helped Ansco to begin to grow into one of the largest employers in the area.

* * * * * *

During this time David had grown into a handsome young man. He had completed his studies at Syracuse University where he was elected President of the National Jewish Fraternity, Zeta Beta Tau. He was Phi Beta Kappa in his studies graduating at the top of his class. Bella and grandmother were extremely proud. Great-Grandfather was heard to say that this could only have happened in America. Where else could a poor immigrant rise to these heights?

Later, David graduated from the Syracuse University School of Law. David reminded everyone of his promise to Abraham. Even though Abraham was in actuality his uncle, David had always known him as his brother because that was the way grandmother had wanted it! He had always looked up to his hero and was always mindful of Abraham's admonition to go to school, get good grades and that the two of then would set up a law practice.

David had attended Syracuse University on an athletic scholarship. His abilities in basketball and baseball had earned him that. David was an outstanding scholar-athlete but academics were foremost in his mind. Not only had he promised Bella that he would make her proud, he reminded himself, every day, of the promise he had made to Abraham.

Upon graduation, David set up a law practice in Binghamton where he lived with his mother, grandmother and great-grandfather. Grandmother was still cleaning houses even though Bella and David had pleaded with her that it wasn't necessary any longer. They told her that they would take care of her. Grandmother's response was always, "And what would I do? I can't leave my families. They depend on me. They treat me with respect, as if I were part of their own families, and not as a stranger who comes to clean."

* * * * * *

The days of the Hoover administration were not the best for the country in the eyes of this up-and-coming attorney. David affiliated himself with the Democratic Party since it was known as the Party of the people while the Republican Party had become known as the Party of Big Business. David became a long-time admirer of Franklin Delano Roosevelt while in law school.

With the inability of the Harding, Coolidge, and Hoover administrations to help the small working class people David had gravitated to the Democratic Party.

David's practice had grown. He was very popular among his working-class neighbors. He always went out of his way to help those in need, sometimes without even receiving any pay for his help. Mama had instilled this mindset into him. She would say, "David, you should never forget where you came from. All of the people around you are hard-working people who care. Don't ever forget!"

When David was asked to run for the office of District Attorney he jumped at the opportunity. Much to the surprise of the political pundits who had predicted a Republican victory in this staunchly Republican area, David won. He was an outstanding District Attorney.

He ran for the office of Mayor and was elected handily. Everyone who had any dealings with David liked his openness and honesty as well as his values of fairness for all. He was especially open-minded when it came to the needs of the minority groups in his city that had grown into quite a large industrial-based and diversified city.

The Republicans were in trouble nationally. The depression that began in 1929 shocked the American people. Unemployment had spread to the point that one-fourth of the work force was without jobs. Banks were in trouble and the savings of many of the working class were wiped out! Public confidence in the American economic system and the government was fading. Binghamton, New York had their share of people in need. Then in 1932, in the midst of the Great Depression three thousand two hundred ten Democratic delegates filled the Chicago Stadium. David was one of them. First, going to Chicago was, for him, like going to another world. Secondly, being in the midst of the wheeler-dealers David was in awe. New York was playing a huge role in the proceedings. In addition to the depression, Prohibition was still a large issue that provoked major debates. After much debate, the delegates voted for the repeal of Prohibition as part of their platform.

But, overshadowing all of this was the concern of the government's responsibility in their role over human welfare.

In that, Franklin Delano Roosevelt promised a New Deal for the people! The idea was attractive to David. After all he had come from working class folks. And, many of the working people in his mother's neighborhood were in dire straits. Roosevelt's platform called for unemployment relief, public works projects and old-age assistance to aid "the forgotten man."

David sat entranced amid the debates and discussions that arose. Despite the fact that Franklin Delano Roosevelt emerged as the candidate with a majority of votes, a number of other candidates held enough votes to prevent him from reaching the two-thirds majority necessary to win. John Nance Garner of Texas, Harry F. Byrd of Virginia and Newton Diehl Baker all stood in Roosevelt's way to victory.

David listened to the political pros in the smoke-filled room called the New York State headquarters. One of the candidates who needed convincing that Roosevelt was the man was Alfred E. Smith also of New York. Smith had made a bid for the presidency in 1928 but lost. Many prognosticators felt his loss came because he was an Irish Catholic. His association with Roman Catholicism was particularly highlighted in the south where Smith was labeled a "Papist Pup." Despite all that, Smith needed to be convinced that he didn't stand a chance in wresting away the republican control over Congress. After a great deal of arm-twisting, Smith capitulated.

Newton Diehl Baker was considered a dark horse candidate. Baker was from West Virginia and had served as Secretary of War under President Woodrow Wilson. Baker was known as a Wilsonian idealist. Baker had attended Johns Hopkins

University and as a student there he met Professor Woodrow Wilson, a visiting lecturer from Princeton. The two became close friends.

After World War I he fought American isolationism and was a strong supporter of the League of Nations. He was known throughout the world as a humanitarian who gave unstintingly of his time and energy in active support of reform groups and charities. In 1928 Baker was appointed to the Hague Tribunal where he distinguished himself as a jurist. Despite all that Baker didn't have the wide support needed to stand in the way of the New York wheeler-dealers.

John Nance Garner had distinguished himself as minority floor leader in the Seventy-first Congress and later as Speaker of the House in the Seventy-second Congress.

Garner was offered the Vice Presidency.

The lengthy "smoke-filled-room" negotiations brought the Texas delegation, led by Sam Rayburn, to the Roosevelt camp. It was felt that Garner could "round out" the ticket by smoothing over the sense that the northern influence, held by the New York "carpetbaggers," controlled everything. Despite all of the back room maneuvering, Roosevelt was still not considered a strong candidate. Nance could bring in the vote from the South and West.

Roosevelt's campaign managers pulled out all of the stops. Working with the convention organizers they were able to successfully arrange the delegates seating so that non-Roosevelt supporters were engulfed amid the Pro-Roosevelt supporters. They also managed to isolate the microphones so that the roar of the crowd favored the Roosevelt supporters. When Roosevelt walked up to the microphone and made his acceptance speech David was enthralled. He was captured by the simplicity of Roosevelt's rhetoric and was captured by the slogans, "New Deal" and "the forgotten man."

David was especially interested in the seemingly new ideas expressed by Roosevelt. He was especially drawn to Roosevelt's New Deal philosophy. Having come from an immigrant family and having grown up among other working-class immigrants, David knew how important programs like social security were.

It was no surprise, then, that the Democratic Party had tapped him as their candidate for the United States Senate to run against the long-time incumbent Senator Richard Woodruff. It was widely known that Woodruff represented the wealthy while David was seen as the man of the people.

It was a nasty campaign that was waged by the Republicans. They came down hard on the fact that David was not married and the fact that David was Jewish. It was intimated that he might be gay. David was also hooked up with all kinds of Zionist movements. His team had all they could do to keep up with and squelch the rumors. They looked at Roosevelt's program as radical and socialist in nature. Yet despite all of the mud-slinging David still commanded a strong following.

On the night of the election, the party faithful gathered in the ballroom of the hotel. It was a happy, confidant crowd. There was loud music, plenty of Utica Club, Fort Schuyler and Rolling Rock beer to wash down the tasty pizza and hors d'oeuvres that were strategically placed throughout the ballroom as the party faithful listened to the election returns over the ballroom loudspeakers. At first, the reports showed the lead to be in the hands of Senator Richard Woodruff. Someone in the audience was heard to say, "That's no surprise. Those votes are all from the "cake-eaters" precincts."

In the meantime, David gathered his mother, grandmother. grandfather, and Miss Westcott along with his chief advisors in a suite several floors above the raucous gathering to listen to the radio as it spewed forth the election results. It was a seemingly long evening. However, it soon became clear that the tide had turned and that David was about to become a United States Senator from Binghamton, New York. His chief advisor told him that it was time to go downstairs to the ballroom and meet with the party faithful. When David and his entourage stepped out of the elevator you could hear whispers of. "He's coming," followed by strains of "For He's A Jolly Good Fellow," and "Happy Days Are Here Again."

David strode up to the dais. When he reached the microphone he began by commending all of the party workers for their hard work. He told them that this victory could not have been possible without the help of all those who passed out pamphlets; those who stuffed envelopes, and those who made telephone calls urging people to vote for him. As he was talking there became a hushed silence over the crowd. Looking to the rear of the room they could see that Senator Richard Woodruff was entering the ballroom and walking toward the dais. He spoke to David. "I wanted to personally congratulate you, Senator on the fine campaign that you waged." "I expect

BELLA

to see good things come out of Washington."

As Senator Woodruff was speaking he had glanced past David and had spotted Bella. He stopped what he was doing and walked over to her. "Bella?" "After all these years I would have known you anywhere. You haven't changed a bit. You're still as beautiful as ever." "But, tell me, what are you doing here? I didn't know you were involved in politics."

Bella looked up and smiled. She responded by saying, "David is my son." Woodruff said, "I didn't know you were married." "May I meet the lucky man?" Bella smiled and said, "No, I never did get married. Together with my parents we raised David to become the man he has become. And now it is time for you to meet your son. David this is your father!" Richard, do you think he will become the Senator that you were?"

Would you like to see your manuscript become a book?

If you are interested in becoming a PublishAmerica author, please submit your manuscript for possible publication to us at:

acquisitions@publishamerica.com

You may also mail in your manuscript to:

**PublishAmerica
PO Box 151
Frederick, MD 21705**

www.publishamerica.com

PublishAmerica

CPSIA information can be obtained at www.ICGtesting.com
Printed in the USA
266212BV00001B/58/P

9 781462 620166